Horatio

The Young Outlaw

Anatiposi

Horatio Alger

The Young Outlaw

Reprint of the original, first published in 1875.

1st Edition 2024 | ISBN: 978-3-38283-272-8

Anatiposi Verlag is an imprint of Outlook Verlagsgesellschaft mbH.

Verlag (Publisher): Outlook Verlag GmbH, Zeilweg 44, 60439 Frankfurt, Deutschland
Vertretungsberechtigt (Authorized to represent): E. Roepke, Zeilweg 44, 60439 Frankfurt, Deutschland
Druck (Print): Books on Demand GmbH, In de Tarpen 42, 22848 Norderstedt, Deutschland

THE YOUNG OUTLAW;

OR,

ADRIFT IN THE STREETS.

BY

HORATIO ALGER, Jr.,

AUTHOR OF "RAGGED DICK,"—"TATTERED TOM,"—"LUCK AND PLUCK,"—"BRAVE AND BOLD," SERIES.

LORING, Publisher,

COR. WASHINGTON AND BROMFIELD STREETS,

BOSTON.

To

MY YOUNG FRIEND,

HARRY L. DE VISSER,

THIS VOLUME

IS

AFFECTIONATELY DEDICATED.

PREFACE.

"THE YOUNG OUTLAW" is the sixth volume of the Tattered Tom Series, and the twelfth of the stories which are wholly or mainly devoted to street-life in New York. The story carries its moral with it, and the writer has little fear that the Young Outlaw will be selected as a model by the boys who may read his adventures, and be amused by the scrapes into which he manages to fall. In previous volumes he has endeavored to show that even a street-boy, by enterprise, industry and integrity, may hope to become a useful and respected citizen. In the present narration he aims to exhibit the opposite side of the picture, and point out the natural consequences of the lack of these qualities.

This may be a proper occasion to express gratitude for the very remarkable favor with which these stories of humble life have been received throughout the country. The writer is glad to believe that they have done something to draw attention to a neglected class of children, whom it is important to elevate and redeem.

NEW YORK, March 25, 1875.

THE YOUNG OUTLAW;

OR,

ADRIFT IN THE STREETS.

CHAPTER I.

THE YOUNG OUTLAW.

"Boy, is this Canal Street?"

The speaker was evidently from the country. He was a tall man, with prominent features, and a face seamed and wrinkled by the passage of nearly seventy years. He wore a rusty cloak, in the style of thirty years gone by, and his clothing generally was of a fashion seldom seen on Broadway.

The boy addressed was leaning against a lamp-post, with both hands in his pockets. His clothes were soiled and ragged, a soft hat, which looked as if it had served in its varied career as a foot-ball, was thrust carelessly on his head. He looked like a genuine representative of the "street Arab," with no thought for to-morrow and its needs, and contented if he could only make sure of a square meal to-day. His face was dirty, and marked by a mingled expression of fun and impudence; but the features were not unpleasing, and, had he been clean and neatly dressed, he would undoubtedly have been considered good-looking.

He turned quickly on being addressed, and started perceptibly, as his glance met the inquiring look of the tall stranger. He seemed at first disposed to run away, but this intention was succeeded by a desire to have some fun with the old man.

"Canal Street's about a mile off. I'll show yer the way for ten cents."

"A mile off? That's strange," said the old man, puzzled. "They told me at the Astor House it was only about ten minutes' walk, straight up."

"That's where you got sold, gov'nor. Give me ten cents, and you won't have no more trouble."

"Are you sure you know Canal Street, yourself?" said the old man, perplexed. "They'd ought to know at the hotel."

"I'd ought to know too. That's where my store is."

"Your store!" ejaculated the old man, fixing his eyes upon his ragged companion, who certainly looked very little like a New York merchant.

"In course. Don't I keep a cigar store at No. 95?"

"I hope you don't smoke yourself," said the deacon (for he was a deacon), solemnly.

"Yes, I do. My constitushun requires it."

"My boy, you are doing a lasting injury to your health," said the old man, impressively.

"Oh, I'm tough. I kin stand it. Better give me a dime, and let me show yer the way."

The deacon was in a hurry to get to Canal Street, and after some hesitation, for he was fond of money, he drew out ten cents, and handed it to his ragged companion.

"There, my boy, show me the way. I should think you might have done it for nothing."

"That aint the way we do business in the city, gov'nor."

"Well, go ahead, I'm in a hurry."

"You needn't be, for *this* is Canal Street," said the boy, edging off a little.

"Then you've swindled me," said the deacon, wrathfully. "Give me back that ten cents."

"Not if I know it," said the boy, mockingly. "That aint the way we do business in the city. I'm goin' to buy two five-cent cigars with that money."

"You said you kept a cigar-store yourself," said the deacon, with sudden recollection.

"You mustn't believe all you hear, gov'nor," said the boy, laughing saucily.

"Well now, if you ain't a bad boy," said the old man.

"What's the odds as long as you're happy?" said the young Arab, carelessly.

Here was a good chance for a moral lesson, and the deacon felt that it was his duty to point out to the young reprobate the error of his ways.

"My young friend," he said, "how can you expect to be happy when you lie and cheat? Such men are never happy."

"Aint they though? You bet I'll be happy when I'm smokin' the two cigars I'm goin' to buy."

"Keep the money, but don't buy the cigars," said the deacon, religion getting the better of his love of money. "Buy yourself some clothes. You appear to need them."

"Buy clo'es with ten cents!" repeated the boy, humorously.

"At any rate, devote the money to a useful purpose, and I shall not mind being cheated out of it. If you keep on this way, you'll end in the gallus."

"That's comin' it rather strong, gov'nor. Hangin's played out in New York. I guess I'm all right."

"I'm afraid you're all wrong, my boy. You're travellin' to destruction."

"Let's change the subject," said the street boy. "You're gittin' personal, and I don't like personal remarks. What'll you bet I can't tell your name?"

"Bet!" ejaculated the deacon, horrified.

"Yes, gov'nor. I'll bet you a quarter I kin tell your name."

"I never bet. It's wicked," said the old man, with emphasis.

"Well, we won't bet, then," said the boy. "Only, if I tell your name right, you give me ten cents. If I don't get it right, I'll give back this dime you gave me. Aint that fair?"

The deacon might have been led to suspect that there was not much difference between the boy's proposal, and the iniquity of a bet, but his mind was rather possessed by the thought that here was a good chance to recover the money out of which he had been so adroitly cheated. Surely there was no wrong in recovering that, as of course he would do, for how could a ragged street boy tell the name of one who lived a hundred and fifty miles distant, in a small country town?

"I'll do it," said the deacon.

"You'll give me ten cents if I tell your name?"

"Yes, and you'll give me back the money I give you if you can't tell."

"That's it, gov'nor."

"Then what's my name, my boy?" and the

deacon extended his hand in readiness to receive the forfeit of a wrong answer.

"Deacon John Hopkins," answered the boy, confidently.

The effect on the old man was startling. He was never more surprised in his life. He stared at the boy open-mouthed, in bewilderment and wonder.

"Well, I declare!" he ejaculated. "I never heard of such a thing."

"Aint I right, gov'nor?"

"Yes, my boy, you're right; but how on earth did you find out?"

"Give me the money, and I'll tell you;" and the boy extended his hand.

The deacon drew the money from his vest-pocket, and handed it to the young Arab, without remonstrance.

"Now tell me, my boy, how you know'd me."

The boy edged off a few feet, then lifted his venerable hat so as to display the whole of his face.

"I'd ought to know you, deacon," he said; "I'm Sam Barker."

"By gracious, if it aint Sam!" ejaculated the old man. "Hallo! stop, I say!"

But Sam was half-way across the street. The deacon hesitated an instant, and then dashed after him, his long cloak floating in the wind, and his hat unconsciously pushed back on the top of his head.

"Stop, you Sam!" he shouted.

But Sam, with his head over his shoulder, already three rods in advance, grinned provokingly, but appeared to have no intention of stopping. The deacon was not used to running, nor did he make due allowance for the difficulty of navigating the crowded streets of the metropolis. He dashed headlong into an apple-stand, and suffered disastrous shipwreck The apple-stand was overturned, the deacon's hat flew off, and he found himself sprawling on the sidewalk, with apples rolling in all directions around him, and an angry dame showering maledictions upon him, and demanding compensation for damages.

The deacon picked himself up, bruised and ashamed, recovered his hat, which had rolled into a mud-puddle, and was forced to pay the woman a dollar before he could get away. When this matter was settled, he looked for Sam, but the boy was out of sight. In fact, he was just around the corner, laughing as if he would split. He had seen his pursuer's discomfiture, and regarded it as a huge practical joke.

"I never had such fun in all my life," he ejaculated, with difficulty, and he went off into a fresh convulsion. "The old feller won't forget me in a hurry."

CHAPTER II.

SAM'S EARLY LIFE.

THREE years before the meeting described in the previous chapter Sam Barker became an orphan, by the death of his father. The father was an intemperate man, and no one grieved much for his death. Sam felt rather relieved than otherwise. He had received many a beating from his father, in his fits of drunken fury, and had been obliged to forage for himself for the most part, getting a meal from one neighbor, a basket of provision from another, and so managed to eke out a precarious subsistence in the tumble-down shanty which he and his father occupied.

Mr. Barker left no will, for the good and sufficient reason that he had no property to dispose of. So, on the day after the funeral, Sam found himself a candidate for the poorhouse. He was a stout boy of twelve, strong and sturdy in spite of insufficient food, and certainly had suffered nothing from luxurious living.

It was a country town in Connecticut, near the Rhode Island border. We will call it Dudley. The selectmen deliberated what should be done with Sam.

"There isn't much for a lad like him to do at the poorhouse," said Major Stebbins. "He'd ought to be set to work. Why don't you take him, Deacon Hopkins?"

"I do need a boy," said the deacon, "but I'm most afeard to take Sam. He's a dreadful mischievous boy, I've heerd."

"He's had a bad example in his father," said the major. "You could train him up the way he'd ought to go."

"Mebbe I could," said the deacon, flattered by this tribute, and reflecting, moreover, that he could get a good deal of work out of Sam without being obliged to pay him wages.

"You could train him up to be a respectable man," said the major. "They wouldn't know what to do with him at the poorhouse."

So the deacon was prevailed upon to take Sam to bring up.

"You're goin' to live with me, Samuel," said the deacon, calling the boy to his side.

"Am I?" asked Sam, surveying the old man attentively.

"Yes; I shall try to make a man of you."

"I'll get to be a man anyway, if I live long enough," said Sam.

"I mean I will make a man of you in a moral sense," explained the deacon.

This, however, was above Sam's comprehension.

"What would you like to do when you're a man?" asked the deacon.

"Smoke a pipe," answered Sam, after some reflection.

The deacon held up his hands in horror.

"What a misguided youth!" he exclaimed. "Can you think of nothing better than to smoke a pipe?"

"Dad liked it," said Sam; "but I guess he liked rum better."

"Your father was a misguided man," said the deacon. "He wasted his substance in riotous living."

"You'd ought to have seen him when he was tight," said Sam, confidentially. "Didn't he tear round then? He'd fling sticks of wood at my head. O jolly! Didn't I run? I used to hide under the bed when I couldn't run out of doors."

"Your father's dead and gone. I don't want to talk against him, but I hope you'll grow up a very different man. Do you think you will like to live with me?"

"I guess so," said Sam. "You live in a good house, where the rain don't leak through the roof on your head. You'll give me lots to eat, too; won't you?"

"You shall have enough," said the deacon, cautiously, "but it is bad to over-eat. Boys ought to be moderate."

"I didn't over-eat to home," said Sam. "I went one day without eatin' a crumb."

"You shall have enough to eat at my house, but you must render a return."

"What's that?"

"You must pay me for it."

"I can't; I aint got a cent."

"You shall pay me in work. He that does not work shall not eat."

"Have I got to work very hard?" asked Sam, anxiously.

"I will not task you beyond your strength, but I shall expect you to work faithfully. I work myself. Everybody works in my house."

Sam was occupied for a brief space in considering the great problem that connects labor and eating. Somehow it didn't seem quite satisfactory.

"I wish I was a pig!" he burst out, rather unexpectedly.

"Why?" demanded the deacon, amazed.

"Pigs have a better time than men and boys. They have all they can eat, and don't have to work for it nuther."

"I'm surprised at you," said the deacon, shocked. "Pigs are only brute animals. They have no souls. Would you be willing to give up your immortal soul for the sake of bein' idle, and doin' no work?"

"I don't know anything 'bout my immortal soul. What good does it do me?" inquired Sam.

"I declare! the boy's actilly gropin' in heathen darkness," said the deacon, beginning to think he had undertaken a tough job.

"What's that?" asked Sam, mystified.

"I haven't time to tell you now, but I must have a long talk with you some day. You aint had no sort of bringing up. Do you ever read the Bible?"

"No, but I've read the life of Cap'n Kidd. He was a smart man, though."

"Captain Kidd, the pirate?" asked the deacon, horrified.

"Yes. Wa'n't he a great man?"

"He calls a pirate a great man!" groaned the deacon.

"I think I'd like to be a pirate," said Sam, admiringly.

"Then you'd die on the gallus!" exclaimed the deacon with energy.

"No, I wouldn't. I wouldn't let 'em catch me," said Sam, confidently.

"I never heerd a boy talk so," said the deacon. "He's as bad as a — a Hottentot."

Deacon Hopkins had no very clear ideas as to the moral or physical condition of Hottentots, or where they lived, but had a general notion that they were in a benighted state, and the comparison seemed to him a good one. Not so to Sam.

"You're calling me names," he said, discontentedly. "You called me a Hottentot."

"I fear you are very much like those poor, benighted creatures, Samuel," said his new guardian; "but it isn't wholly your fault. You have never had any religious or moral instruction. This must be rectified. I shall buy you a catechism this very day."

"Will you?" asked Sam, eagerly, who, it must be explained, had an idea that a catechism was something good to eat.

"Yes, I'll stop at the store and get one."

They went into Pendleton's store, — a general country variety store, in which the most dissimilar articles were kept for sale.

"Have you got a catechism?" asked the deacon, entering with Sam at his side.

"We've got just one left."

"How much is it?"

"Ten cents."

"I'll take it."

Sam looked on with interest till the clerk produced the article; then his countenance underwent a change.

"Why, it's a book," he said.

"Of course it is. It is a very good book, from which you will learn all about your duty, and your religious obligations."

"You needn't buy it. I don't want it," said Sam.

"Don't want the catechism!" said the deacon, not without anger.

"No, it aint any good."

"My boy, I know better what is good for you than you do. I shall buy you the catechism."

"I'd rather you'd get me that book," said Sam, pointing to a thin pamphlet copy of "Jack, the Giant-Killer."

But Deacon Hopkins persisted in making the purchase proposed.

"Are there any pictures in it?" asked Sam.

"No."

"Then I shan't like it."

"You don't know what is for your good. I hope you will be wiser in time. But here we are at the house. Come right in, and mind you wipe your feet."

This was Sam's first introduction into the Hopkins' household. He proved a disturbing element, as we shall presently see.

CHAPTER III.

A HARD CASE.

The first meal to which Sam sat down at the deacon's house was supper. It was only a plain supper, — tea, bread and butter, and apple-pie; but to Sam, who was not used to regular meals of any kind, it seemed luxurious. He despatched slice after slice of bread, eating twice as much as any one else at the table, and after eating his share of the pie gazed hungrily at the single slice which remained on the plate, and asked for that also.

Deacon Hopkins thought it was time to interfere.

"You've had one piece a'ready," he said.

"I know it," said Sam; "but I'm hungry."

"I don't see how you can be. You've eat more than any of us."

"It takes a good deal to fill me up," said Sam, frankly.

"The boy'll eat us out of house and home," said Mrs. Hopkins, in alarm. "You can't have any more. You've had enough."

Sam withdrew his plate. He did not look abashed, for he was never much inclined that way, nor did his feelings appear to be hurt, for he was not sensitive; but he took the matter coolly, and pushing back his chair from the table was about to leave the room.

"Where are you a-goin'?" asked his new guardian.

"Out doors."

"Stop. I've got something for you to do."

The deacon went to the mantel-piece and took therefrom the catechism.

"You aint had no bringin' up, Samuel," he said. "You don't know nothin' about your moral and religious obligations. It's my dooty to make you learn how to walk uprightly."

"I can walk straight now," said Sam.

"I don't mean that—I mean in a moral sense. Come here."

Sam unwillingly drew near the deacon.

"Here, I want you to study the first page of the catechism, and recite it to me before you go to bed."

Sam took the book, and looked at the first page doubtfully.

"What's the good of it?" he demanded, in a discontented voice.

"What's the good of the catechism?" exclaimed the deacon, shocked. "It'll l'arn you your duties. It'll benefit your immortal soul."

"I don't care if it will," said Sam, perversely. "What do I care about my soul? It never did me no good."

"Did you ever see such a heathen, Martha?" said the deacon, in despair, turning to his wife.

"You'll be sorry you ever took him," said Mrs. Hopkins, shaking her head.

"Set down in the corner, and l'arn your lesson, Samuel," said the old man.

Sam looked undecided whether to obey or not, but under the circumstances he thought it best to obey. He began to read the catechism, but it did not interest him. His eyes were not long fixed on the

of freedom. He did not mean to return till it was too late to study the catechism any longer.

"What's the use of wearin' out a feller's eyes over such stuff?" he thought.

It is not necessary to follow Sam's movements through the evening. At nine o'clock he opened the front door, and went in, not exactly abashed, but uncertain how the deacon would receive him.

Deacon Hopkins had his steel-bowed spectacles on, and was engaged in reading a good book. He looked up sternly as Sam entered.

"Samuel, where have you been?" he asked.

"Out in the woods," said Sam, coolly.

"Didn't I tell you to get your catechism?" demanded the old man, sternly.

"So I did," said Sam, without blushing.

"I am afraid you are telling a lie. Mrs. Hopkins said she went out of the room a minute, and when she came back you were gone. Is that so?"

"Yes, I guess so," said Sam.

"Then how did you have time to l'arn your lesson?"

"It wasn't long," muttered Sam.

"Come here, and I will see if you know anything about it."

The deacon took the book, laid it flat on his lap, and read out the first question, looking inquiringly at Sam for the answer.

Sam hesitated, and scratched his head. "I give it up," said he.

"Do you think I am askin' conundrums?" said the deacon, sternly.

"No," said Sam, honestly.

"Why don't you know?"

"Because I can't tell."

"Because you didn't study it. Aint you ashamed of your ignorance?"

"What's the use of knowin'?"

"It is *very* important," said the deacon, impressively. "Now I will ask you the next question."

Sam broke down, and confessed that he didn't know.

"Then you told me a lie. You said you studied the lesson."

"I didn't understand it."

"Then you should have studied longer. Don't you know it is wicked to lie?"

"A feller can't tell the truth all the time," said Sam, as if he were stating a well-known fact.

"Certainly he can," said the deacon. "I always do."

"Do you?" inquired Sam, regarding the old man with curiosity.

"Of course. It is every one's duty to tell the truth. You ought to die rather than tell a lie. I have read of a man who was threatened with death. He might have got off if he had told a lie. But he wouldn't."

"Did he get killed?" asked Sam, with interest.

"Yes."

"Then he must have been a great fool," said Sam, contemptuously. "You wouldn't catch me makin' such a fool of myself."

"He was a noble man," said the deacon, indignantly. "He laid down his life for the truth."

"What good did it do?" said Sam.

"I am afraid, Samuel, you are in a very benighted condition. You appear to have no conceptions of duty."

"I guess I haven't," said Sam. "I dunno what they are."

"It is all the more necessary that you should study your catechism. I shall expect you to get the same lesson to-morrow evenin'. It's too late to study now."

"So it is," said Sam, with alacrity.

"I will show you where you are to sleep. You must get up airly to go to work. I will come and wake you up."

Sam was not overjoyed at this announcement. It did not strike him that he should enjoy going to work early in the morning. However, he felt instinctively that it would do no good to argue the matter at present, and he followed the deacon upstairs in silence. He was ushered into a small room partitioned off from the attic.

"You'll sleep there," said the deacon, pointing to a cot-bed in the corner. "I'll call you at five o'clock to-morrow mornin'."

Sam undressed himself, and got into bed.

"This is jolly," thought he; "a good deal better than at home. If it warn't for that plaguey catechism, I'd like livin' here fust-rate. I wish I had another piece of that pie."

In ten minutes Sam was fast asleep; but the deacon was not so fortunate. He lay awake a long time, wondering in perplexity what he should do to reform the young outlaw of whom he had taken charge.

"He's a cur'us boy," thought the good man. "Seems to have no more notion of religion than a Choctaw or a Hottentot. An' yet he's been livin' in a Christian community all his life. I'm afeared he takes after his father."

CHAPTER IV.

SAM FRIGHTENS THE HOUSEHOLD.

SAM usually slept the whole night through; but to-night was an exception. It might have been because he was in a strange bed, and in a strange house. At any rate, he woke in time to hear the clock on the church, of which his guardian was deacon, strike two.

"Where am I?" was his first thought.

He remembered almost immediately, and the thought made him broad awake. He ought not to have been hungry at that hour, and in fact he was not, but the thought of the pie forced itself upon his mind, and he felt a longing for the slice that was left over from supper. Quick upon this thought came another, "Why couldn't he creep downstairs softly, and get it? The deacon and his wife were fast asleep, Who would find him out?"

A boy better brought up than Sam might have reflected that it was wrong; but, as the deacon said,

Sam had no "conceptions of duty," or, more properly, his conscience was not very active. He got out of bed, slipped on his stockings, and crept softly downstairs, feeling his way. It was very dark, for the entries were unlighted, but finally he reached the kitchen without creating any alarm.

Now for the closet. It was not locked, and Sam opened the door without difficulty.

"I wish I had a match, so's to see where the pie is," he thought.

He felt around, but the pie must have been placed elsewhere, for he could not find it. It had really been placed on the highest shelf, which Sam had not as yet explored. But there are dangers in feeling around in the dark. Our hero managed to dislodge a pile of plates, which fell with a crash upon his feet. There was a loud crash of broken crockery, and the noise was increased by the howls of Sam, who danced up and down with pain.

The noise reached the chamber where the deacon and his wife were calmly reposing. Mrs. Hopkins was a light sleeper, and was awakened at once.

She was startled and terrified, and, sitting up in bed, shook her husband violently by the shoulder.

"Deacon — Deacon Hopkins!" she exclaimed.

"What's the matter?" asked the deacon, drowsily.

"Matter enough. There's robbers downstairs."

Now the deacon was broad awake.

"Robbers!" he exclaimed. "Pooh! Nonsense! You're dreamin', wife."

Just then there was another racket. Sam, in trying to effect his escape, tumbled over a chair, and there was a yell of pain.

"Am I dreaming now, deacon?" demanded his wife, triumphantly.

"You're right, wife," said the deacon, turning pale, and trembling. "It's an awful situation. What shall we do?"

"Do? Go downstairs, and confront the villains!" returned his wife, energetically.

"They might shoot me," said her husband, panic-stricken. "They're — they're said to be very desperate fellows."

"Are you a man, and won't defend your property?" exclaimed his wife, taunting him. "Do you want *me* to go down?"

"Perhaps you'd better," said the deacon, accepting the suggestion with alacrity.

"What!" shrieked Mrs. Hopkins. "You are willing they should shoot me?"

"They wouldn't shoot a woman," said the deacon.

But his wife was not appeased.

Just then the unlucky Sam trod on the tail of the cat, who was quietly asleep on the hearth. With the instinct of self-defence, she scratched his leg, which was undefended by the customary clothing, and our hero, who did not feel at all heroic in the dark, not knowing what had got hold of him, roared with pain and fright.

"This is terrible!" gasped the deacon. "Martha, is the door locked?"

"No."

"Then I'll get up and lock it. O Lord, what will become of us?"

Sam was now ascending the stairs, and, though he tried to walk softly, the stairs creaked beneath his weight.

"They're comin' upstairs," exclaimed Mrs. Hopkins. "Lock the door quick, deacon, or we shall be murdered in our bed."

The deacon reached the door in less time than he would have accomplished the same feat in the day-time, and hurriedly locked it.

"It's locked, Martha," he said, "but they may break it down."

"Or fire through the door —"

"Let's hide under the bed," suggested the heroic deacon.

"Don't speak so loud. They'll hear. I wish it was mornin'."

The deacon stood at the door listening, and made a discovery.

"They're goin' up into the garret," he announced. "That's strange —"

"What do they want up there, I wonder?"

"They can't think we've got anything valuable up there."

"Deacon," burst out Mrs. Hopkins, with a sudden idea, "I believe we've been fooled."

"Fooled! What do you mean?"

"I believe it isn't robbers."

"Not robbers? Why, you told me it was," said her husband, bewildered.

"*I believe it's that boy.*"

"What, — Sam?"

"Yes."

"What would he want downstairs?"

"I don't know, but it's him, I'll be bound. Light the lamp, deacon, and go up and see."

"But it might be robbers," objected the deacon, in alarm. "They might get hold of me, and kill me."

"I didn't think you were such a coward, *Mr.* Hopkins," said his wife, contemptuously. When she indulged in severe sarcasm, she was accustomed to omit her husband's title.

"I aint a coward, but I don't want to risk my life. It's a clear flyin' in the face of Providence. You'd ought to see that it is, Martha," said the deacon, reproachfully.

"I don't see it. I see that you are frightened, that's what I see. Light the lamp, and I'll go up myself."

"Well, Martha, it's better for you to go. They won't touch a woman."

He lighted the lamp, and his wife departed on her errand. It might have been an unconscious action on the part of the deacon, but he locked the door after his wife.

Mrs. Hopkins proceeded to the door of Sam's bed-chamber, and, as the door was unfastened, she entered. Of course he was still awake, but he pretended to be asleep.

"Sam," said Mrs. Hopkins.

There was a counterfeited snore.

"Sam — say!"

Sam took no notice.

The lady took him by the shoulder, and shook him with no gentle hand, so that our hero was compelled to rouse himself.

"What's up?" he asked, rubbing his eyes in apparent surprise.

"I am," said Mrs. Hopkins, shortly, "and you have been."

"I!" protested Sam, innocently. "Why, I was

sound asleep when you came in. I don't know what's been goin' on. Is it time to get up?"

"What have you been doing downstairs?" demanded Mrs. Hopkins, sternly.

"Who says I've been downstairs?" asked Sam.

"I'm sure you have. I heard you."

"It must have been somebody else."

"There is no one else to go down. Neither the deacon nor myself has been down."

"Likely it's thieves."

But Mrs. Hopkins felt convinced, from Sam's manner, that he was the offender, and she determined to make him confess it.

"Get up," she said, "and go down with me."

"I'm sleepy," objected Sam.

"So am I, but I mean to find out all about this matter."

Sam jumped out of bed, and unwillingly accompanied Mrs. Hopkins downstairs. The latter stopped at her own chamber-door, and tried to open it.

"Who's there?" asked the deacon, tremulously.

"I am," said his wife, emphatically.

"So you locked the door on your wife, did you,

because you thought there was danger. It does you great credit, upon my word."

"What have you found out?" asked her husband, evading the reproach. "Was it Sam that made all the noise?"

"How could I," said Sam, "when I was fast asleep?"

"I'm goin' to take him down with me to see what mischief's done," said Mrs. Hopkins. "Do you want to go too?"

The deacon, after a little hesitation, followed his more courageous spouse, — at a safe distance, however, — and the three entered the kitchen, which had been the scene of Sam's noisy exploits. It showed traces of his presence in an overturned chair. Moreover, the closet-door was wide open, and broken pieces of crockery were scattered over the floor.

A light dawned upon Mrs. Hopkins. She had solved the mystery!

CHAPTER V.

SAM COMBINES BUSINESS WITH PLEASURE.

"You came down after that pie," she said, turning upon Sam.

"What pie?" asked Sam, looking guilty, however.

"Don't ask me. You know well enough. You couldn't find it in the dark, and that's the way you came to make such a noise. Ten of my nice plates broken, too! What do you say to that, Deacon Hopkins?"

"Samuel," said the deacon, "did you do this wicked thing?"

A moment's reflection convinced Sam that it would be idle to deny it longer. The proofs of his guilt were too strong. He might have plead in his defence "emotional insanity," but he was not familiar with the course of justice in New York. He was, however, fertile in expedients, and thought of the next best thing.

"Mebbe I walked in my sleep," he admitted.

"Did you ever walk in your sleep?" asked the deacon, hastily.

"Lots of times," said Sam.

"It is rather strange you should go to the closet in your sleep," said Mrs. Hopkins, suspiciously. "I suppose, if you'd found it, you'd have eaten it in your sleep."

"Likely I should," said Sam. "I was dreamin' of the pie. You know how to make pie, Mrs. Hopkins; I never tasted so good before."

Mrs. Hopkins was not a soft woman, but she was proud of her cooking, and accessible to flattery on that subject. Sam could not have defended himself better.

"That may be," she said, "about your walking in your sleep; but once is enough. Hereafter I'll lock your door on the outside. I can't be waked up every night, nor I can't have my plates broken."

"S'pose the house should catch fire," suggested Sam, who didn't fancy being locked up in his room.

"If it does, I'll come and let you out. The house is safer when you're safe in bed."

"My wife is right, Samuel," said the deacon,

recovering his dignity now that his fears were removed. "You must be locked in after to-night."

Sam did not reply. On the whole, he felt glad to get off so well, after alarming the house so seriously.

"Do you mean to stay downstairs all night, Deacon Hopkins?" demanded his wife, with uncalled-for asperity. "If so, I shall leave you to yourself."

"I'm ready to go up when you are," said her husband. "I thought you mightn't feel like stayin' down here alone."

"Much protection you'd be in time of danger, Mr. Hopkins, — you that locked the door on your wife, because you was afraid!"

"I wasn't thinkin'," stammered the deacon.

"Probably not," said his wife, in an incredulous tone. "Now go up. It's high time we were all in bed again."

Sam was not called at as early an hour as the deacon intended. The worthy man, in consequence of his slumbers being interrupted, overslept himself, and it was seven o'clock when he called Sam.

"Get up, Samuel," he said; "it's dreadful late,

and you must be spry, or you won't catch up with the work."

Work, however, was not prominent in Sam's mind, as his answer showed.

"Is breakfast ready?" he asked, rubbing his eyes.

"It's most ready. Get right up, for it's time to go to work."

"I 'spose we'll have breakfast first," said Sam.

"If it's ready."

Under these circumstances, Sam did not hurry. He did not care to work before breakfast, nor, for that matter, afterwards, if he could help it. So he made a leisurely, though not an elaborate toilet, and did not come down till Mrs. Hopkins called sharply up the attic stairs, "Come down, you Sam!"

"All right, ma'am, I'm comin'," said Sam, who judged rightly that breakfast was ready.

"We shan't often let you sleep so late," said Mrs. Hopkins, who sat behind the waiter. "We were broken of our rest through your cutting up last night, and so we overslept ourselves."

"It's pretty early," said Sam.

"We'd ought to have been at work in the field an hour ago," said the deacon.

At the table Sam found work that suited him better.

"You've got a good appetite," said Mrs. Hopkins, as Sam took the seventh slice of bread.

"I most generally have," said Sam, with his mouth full.

"That's encouraging, I'm sure," said Mrs. Hopkins, drily.

There was no pie on the table, as Sam noticed, to his regret. However, he was pretty full when he rose from the table.

"Now, Samuel, you may come along with me," said the deacon, putting on his hat.

Sam followed him out to the barn, where, in one corner, were kept the hoes, rakes, and other farming implements in use.

"Here's a hoe for you," said the deacon.

"What are we going to do?" asked Sam.

"The potatoes need hoeing. Did you ever hoe potatoes?"

"No."

"You'll l'arn. It aint hard."

The field was some little distance from the house, — a two-acre lot wholly devoted to potatoes.

"I guess we'll begin at the further corner," said the deacon. "Come along."

When they had reached the part of the field specified, the deacon stopped.

"Now," said he, "just see how I do it;" and he carefully hoed around one of the hills.

"There, you see it's easy."

"I guess I can do it. Are you goin' to stay here?"

"No, I've got to go to the village, to the blacksmith's. I'll be back in about two hours. Jest hoe right along that row, and then come back again on the next. Do you understand?"

"Yes," said Sam.

"I want you to work as spry as you can, so's to make up for lost time."

"What time do you have dinner?" asked our hero.

"You aint hungry *so* quick, be you?"

"No, but I shall be bimeby. I thought I'd like to know when to quit work, and go to dinner."

"I'll be back before that. You needn't worry about that."

The deacon turned, and directed his steps homeward.

As long as he was in sight Sam worked with tolerable speed. But when the tall and stooping figure had disappeared from view he rested, and looked around him.

"It'll be a sight of work to hoe all them potatoes," he said to himself. "I wonder if the old man expects me to do the whole. It'll be a tough job."

Sam leisurely hoed another hill.

"It's gettin' hot," he said. "Why don't they have trees to give shade? Then it would be more comfortable."

He hoed another hill, taking a little longer time.

"I guess there must be a million hills," he reflected, looking around him thoughtfully. "It'll take me from now till next winter to hoe 'em all."

At the rate Sam was working, his calculation of the time it would take him was not far out probably.

He finished another hill.

Just then a cat, out on a morning walk, chanced to pass through the field a few rods away. Now Sam could never see a cat without wanting to chase it, — a fact which would have led the cat, had she been aware of it, to give him a wide berth. But, unluckily, Sam saw her.

"Scat!" he exclaimed, and, grasping his hoe, he ran after puss.

The cat took alarm, and, climbing the wall which separated the potato-field from the next, sped over it in terror. Sam followed with whoops and yells, which served to accelerate her speed. Occasionally he picked up a stone, and threw at her, and once he threw the hoe in the excitement of his chase. But four legs proved more than a match for two, and finally he was obliged to give it up, but not till he had run more than quarter of a mile. He sat down to rest on a rock, and soon another boy came up, with a fishing-pole over his shoulder.

"What are you doing, Sam?" he asked.

"I've been chasin' a cat," said Sam.

"Didn't catch her, did you?"

"No, hang it."

"Where'd you get that hoe?"

"I'm to work for Deacon Hopkins. He's took me. Where are you goin'?"

"A-fishing."

"I wish I could go."

"So do I. I'd like company."

"Where are you goin' to fish?"

"In a brook close by, down at the bottom of this field."

"I'll go and look on a minute or two. I guess there isn't any hurry about them potatoes."

The minute or two lengthened to an hour and a half, when Sam roused himself from his idle mood, and shouldering his hoe started for the field where he had been set to work.

It was full time. The deacon was there before him, surveying with angry look the half-dozen hills, which were all that his young assistant had thus far hoed.

"Now there'll be a fuss," thought Sam, and he was not far out in that calculation.

CHAPTER VI.

SAM'S SUDDEN SICKNESS.

"WHERE have you been, you young scamp?" demanded the deacon, wrathfully.

"I just went away a minute or two," said Sam, abashed.

"A minute or two!" ejaculated the deacon.

"It may have been more," said Sam. "You see I aint got no watch to tell time by."

"How comes it that you have only got through six hills all the morning?" said the deacon, sternly.

"Well, you see, a cat came along —" Sam began to explain.

"What if she did?" interrupted the deacon. "She didn't stop your work, did she?"

"Why, I thought I'd chase her out of the field."

"What for?"

"I thought she might scratch up some of the potatoes," said Sam, a brilliant excuse dawning upon him.

"How long did it take you to chase her out of the field, where she wasn't doing any harm?"

"I was afraid she'd come back, so I chased her a good ways."

"Did you catch her?"

"No, but I drove her away. I guess she won't come round here again," said Sam, in the tone of one who had performed a virtuous action.

"Did you come right back?"

"I sat down to rest. You see I was pretty tired with running so fast."

"If you didn't run any faster than you have worked, a snail would catch you in half a minute," said the old man, with justifiable sarcasm. "Samuel, your excuse is good for nothing. I must punish you."

Sam stood on his guard, prepared to run if the deacon should make hostile demonstrations. But his guardian was not a man of violence, and did not propose to inflict blows. He had another punishment in view suited to Sam's particular case.

"I'll go right to work," said Sam, seeing that no violence was intended, and hoping to escape the punishment threatened, whatever it might be.

"You'd better," said the deacon.

Our hero (I am afraid he has not manifested any heroic qualities as yet) went to work with remarkable energy, to the imminent danger of the potato-tops, which he came near uprooting in several instances.

"Is this fast enough?" he asked.

"It'll do. I'll take the next row, and we'll work along together. Take care, — I don't want the potatoes dug up."

They kept it up for an hour or more, Sam working more steadily, probably, than he had ever done before in his life. He began to think it was no joke, as he walked from hill to hill, keeping up with the deacon's steady progress.

"There aint much fun about this," he thought. "I don't like workin' on a farm. It's awful tiresome."

"What's the use of hoein' potatoes?" he asked, after a while. "Won't they grow just as well without it?"

"No," said the deacon.

"I don't see why not."

"They need to have the earth loosened around them, and heaped up where it's fallen away."

"It's a lot of trouble," said Sam.

"We must all work," said the deacon, sententiously.

"I wish potatoes growed on trees like apples," said Sam. "They wouldn't be no trouble then."

"You mustn't question the Almighty's doin's, Samuel," said the deacon, seriously. "Whatever he does is right."

"I was only wonderin', that was all," said Sam.

"Human wisdom is prone to err," said the old man, indulging in a scrap of proverbial philosophy.

"What does that mean?" thought Sam, carelessly hitting the deacon's foot with his descending hoe. Unfortunately, the deacon had corns on that foot, and the blow cost him a sharp twinge.

"You careless blockhead!" he shrieked, raising the injured foot from the ground, while a spasm of anguish contracted his features. "Did you take my foot for a potato-hill?"

"Did I hurt you?" asked Sam, innocently.

"You hurt me like thunder," gasped the deacon,

using, in his excitement, words which in calmer moments he would have avoided.

"I didn't think it was your foot," said Sam.

"I hope you'll be more careful next time; you most killed me."

"I will," said Sam.

"I wonder if it isn't time for dinner," he began to think presently, but, under the circumstances, thought it best not to refer to the matter. But at last the welcome sound of the dinner-bell was heard, as it was vigorously rung at the back door by Mrs. Hopkins.

"That's for dinner, Samuel," said the deacon. "We will go to the house."

"All right!" said Sam, with alacrity, throwing down the hoe in the furrow.

"Pick up that hoe, and carry it with you," said the deacon.

"Then we won't work here any more to-day!" said Sam, brightening up.

"Yes, we will; but it's no way to leave the hoe in the fields. Some cat might come along and steal it," he added, with unwonted sarcasm.

Sam laughed as he thought of the idea of a cat

stealing a hoe, and the deacon smiled at his own joke.

Dinner was on the table. It was the fashion there to put all on at once, and Sam, to his great satisfaction, saw on one side a pie like that which had tempted him the night before. The deacon saw his look, and it suggested a fitting punishment. But the time was not yet.

Sam did ample justice to the first course of meat and potatoes. When that was despatched, Mrs. Hopkins began to cut the pie.

The deacon cleared his throat.

"Samuel is to have no pie, Martha," he said.

His wife thought it was for his misdeeds of the night before, and so did Sam.

"I couldn't help walkin' in my sleep," he said, with a blank look of disappointment.

"It aint that," said the deacon.

"What is it, then?" asked his wife.

"Samuel ran away from his work this mornin', and was gone nigh on to two hours," said her husband.

"You are quite right, Deacon Hopkins," said his

wife, emphatically. "He don't deserve any dinner at all."

"Can't I have some pie?" asked Sam, who could not bear to lose so tempting a portion of the repast.

"No, Samuel. What I say I mean. He that will not work shall not eat."

"I worked hard enough afterwards," muttered Sam.

"After I came back—yes, I know that. You worked well part of the time, so I gave you part of your dinner. Next time let the cats alone."

"Can I have some more meat, then?" asked Sam.

"Ye-es," said the deacon, hesitating. "You need strength to work this afternoon."

"S'pose I get that catechism this afternoon instead of goin' to work," suggested Sam.

"That will do after supper, Samuel. All things in their place. The afternoon is for work; the evening for readin' and study, and improvin' the mind."

Sam reflected that the deacon was a very obstinate man, and decided that his arrangements were very foolish. What was the use of living if you'd got to work all the time? A good many people, older than

Sam, are of the same opinion, and it is not wholly without reason; but then, it should be borne in mind that Sam was opposed to all work. He believed in enjoying himself, and the work might take care of itself. But how could it be avoided?

As Sam was reflecting, a way opened itself. He placed his hand on his stomach, and began to roll his eyes, groaning meanwhile.

"What's the matter?" asked Mrs. Hopkins.

"I feel sick," said Sam, screwing up his face into strange contortions.

"It's very sudden," said Mrs. Hopkins, suspiciously.

"So 'tis," said Sam. "I'm afraid I'm going to be very sick. Can I lay down?"

"What do you think it is, Martha?" asked the deacon, looking disturbed.

"I know what it is," said his wife, calmly. "I've treated such attacks before. Yes, you may lay down in your room, and I'll bring you some tea, as soon as I can make it."

"All right," said Sam, elated at the success of his

little trick. It was very much pleasanter to lie down than to hoe potatoes on a hot day.

"How easy I took in the old woman!" he thought.

It was not long before he changed his mind, as we shall see in the next chapter.

CHAPTER VII.

SAM MEETS HIS MATCH.

SAM went upstairs with alacrity, and lay down on the bed, — not that he was particularly tired, but because he found it more agreeable to lie down than to work in the field.

"I wish I had something to read," he thought, — "some nice dime novel like 'The Demon of the Danube.' That was splendid. I like it a good deal better than Dickens. It's more excitin'."

But there was no library in Sam's room, and it was very doubtful whether there were any dime novels in the house. The deacon belonged to the old school of moralists, and looked with suspicion upon all works of fiction, with a very few exceptions, such as Pilgrim's Progress, and Robinson Crusoe, which, however, he supposed to be true stories.

Soon Sam heard the step of Mrs. Hopkins on the

stairs. He immediately began to twist his features in such a way as to express pain.

Mrs. Hopkins entered the room with a cup of hot liquid in her hand.

"How do you feel?" she asked.

"I feel bad," said Sam.

"Are you in pain?"

"Yes, I've got a good deal of pain."

"Whereabouts?"

Sam placed his hand on his stomach, and looked sad.

"Yes, I know exactly what is the matter with you," said the deacon's wife.

"Then you know a good deal," thought Sam, "for I don't know of anything at all myself."

This was what he thought, but he said, "Do you?"

"Oh, yes; I've had a good deal of experience. I know what is good for you."

Sam looked curiously at the cup.

"What is it?" he asked.

"It's hot tea; it's very healin'."

Sam supposed it to be ordinary tea, and he had

no objection to take it. But when he put it to his lips there was something about the odor that did not please him.

"It doesn't smell good," he said, looking up in the face of Mrs. Hopkins.

"Medicine generally doesn't," she said, quietly.

"I thought it was tea," said Sam.

"So it is; it is wormwood-tea."

"I don't think I shall like it," hesitated Sam.

"No matter if you don't, it will do you good," said Mrs. Hopkins.

Sam tasted it, and his face assumed an expression of disgust.

"I can't drink it," he said.

"You must," said Mrs. Hopkins, firmly.

"I guess I'll get well without," said our hero, feeling that he was in a scrape.

"No, you won't. You're quite unwell. I can see it by your face."

"Can you?" said Sam, beginning to be alarmed about his health.

"You must take this tea," said the lady, firmly.

"I'd rather not."

"That's neither here nor there. The deacon needs you well, so you can go to work, and this will cure you as quick as anything."

"Suppose it doesn't?" said Sam.

"Then I shall bring you up some castor-oil in two hours."

Castor-oil! This was even worse than wormwood tea, and Sam's heart sank within him.

"The old woman's too much for me," he thought, with a sigh.

"Come, take the tea," said Mrs. Hopkins. "I can't wait here all day."

Thus adjured, Sam made a virtue of necessity, and, shutting his eyes, gulped down the wormwood. He shuddered slightly when it was all done, and his face was a study.

"Well done!" said Mrs. Hopkins. "It's sure to do you good."

"I think I'd have got well without," said Sam. "I'm afraid it won't agree with me."

"If it don't," said Mrs. Hopkins, cheerfully, "I'll try some castor-oil."

"I guess I won't need it," said Sam, hastily.

"It was awful," said Sam to himself, as his nurse left him alone. "I'd rather hoe potatoes than take it again. I never see such a terrible old woman. She would make me do it, when I wasn't no more sick than she is."

Mrs. Hopkins smiled to herself as she went downstairs.

"Served him right," she said to herself. "I'll l'arn him to be sick. Guess he won't try it again very soon."

Two hours later Mrs. Hopkins presented herself at Sam's door. He had been looking out of the window; but he bundled into bed as soon as he heard her. Appearances must be kept up.

"How do you feel now, Sam?" asked Mrs. Hopkins.

"A good deal better," said Sam, surveying in alarm a cup of some awful decoction in her hand.

"Do you feel ready to go to work again?"

"Almost," said Sam, hesitating.

"The wormwood-tea did you good, it seems; but you're not quite well yet."

"I'll soon be well," said Sam, hastily.

"I mean you shall be," said his visitor. "I've brought you some more medicine."

"Is it tea?"

"No, castor-oil."

"I don't need it," said Sam, getting up quickly. "I'm well."

"If you are not well enough to go to work, you must take some oil."

"Yes, I am," said Sam. "I'll go right out into the field."

"I don't want you to go unless you are quite recovered. I'm sure the oil will bring you 'round."

"I'm all right, now," said Sam, hastily.

"Very well; if you think so, you can go to work."

Rather ruefully Sam made his way to the potato-field, with his hoe on his shoulder.

"Tea and castor-oil are worse than work," he thought. "The old woman's got the best of me, after all. I wonder whether she knew I was makin' believe."

On this point Sam could not make up his mind. She certainly seemed in earnest, and never expressed a doubt about his being really sick. But all the same, she made sickness very disagreeable to him, and he felt that in future he should not pretend sickness when she was at home. It made him almost sick to think of the bitter tea he had already drunk, and the oil would have been even worse.

The deacon looked up as he caught sight of Sam.

"Have you got well?" he asked innocently, for he had not been as clear-sighted as his wife in regard to the character of Sam's malady.

"Yes," said Sam, "I'm a good deal better, but I don't feel quite so strong as I did."

"Mebbe it would be well for you to fast a little," said the deacon, in all sincerity, for fasting was one of his specifics in case of sickness.

"No, I don't think it would, said Sam, quickly. "I'll feel better by supper-time."

"I hope you will," said the deacon.

"I wish I had a piece of pie or somethin' to take the awful taste out of my mouth," thought Sam. "I can taste that wormwood jist as plain! I wonder why such things are allowed to grow."

For the rest of the afternoon Sam worked unusally well. He was under the the deacon's eye, and unable to get away, though he tried at least once. After they had been at work for about an hour, Sam said suddenly, "Don't you feel thirsty, Deacon Hopkins?"

"What makes you ask?" said the deacon.

"Because I'd jist as lieves go to the house and get some water," said Sam, with a very obliging air.

"You're very considerate, Samuel; but I don't think it's healthy to drink between meals."

"Supposin' you're thirsty," suggested Sam, disappointed.

"It's only fancy. You don't need drink railly. You only think you do," said the deacon, and he made some further remarks on the subject to which Sam listened discontentedly. He began to think his situation a very hard one.

"It's work — work all the time," he said to himself. "What's the good of workin' yourself to death? When I'm a man I'll work only when I want to."

Sam did not consider that there might be some difficulty in earning a living unless he were willing to work for it. The present discomfort was all he thought of.

At last, much to Sam's joy, the deacon gave the signal to return to the house.

"If you hadn't been sick, we'd have got through more, he said; "but to-morrow we must make up for lost time."

"I hope it'll rain to-morrow," thought Sam. "We can't work in the rain."

At supper the wormwood seemed to give him additional appetite.

"I'm afraid you'll make yourself sick again, Samuel," said the deacon.

"There aint no danger," said Sam, looking alarmed at the suggestion. "I feel all right now."

"The wormwood did you good," said Mrs. Hopkins, drily.

"I wonder if she means anything," thought Sam

CHAPTER VIII.

SAM'S TEMPTATION.

A MONTH passed, a month which it is safe to say was neither satisfactory to Sam for his employer. The deacon discovered that the boy needed constant watching. When he was left to himself, he was sure to shirk his work, and indulge his natural love of living at ease. His appetite showed no signs of decrease, and the deacon was led to remark that "Samuel had the stiddyest appetite of any boy he ever knew. He never seemed to know when he had eaten enough."

As for Mrs. Hopkins, Sam failed to produce a fovorable impression upon her. He was by no means her ideal of a boy, though it must be added that this ideal was so high that few living boys could expect to attain it. He must have an old head on young shoulders, and in fact be an angel in all respects except the wings. On these Mrs. Hopkins probably would not insist. Being only a boy, and considerably lazier and more mischievous than the average, there was not much prospect of Sam's satisfying her requirements.

"You'd better send him to the poorhouse, deacon," she said more than once. "He's the most shif'less boy I ever see, and it's awful the amount he eats."

"I guess I'll try him a leetle longer," said the deacon. "He aint had no sort of bringin' up, you know."

So at the end of four weeks Sam still continued a member of the deacon's household.

As for Sam, things were not wholly satisfactory to him. In spite of all his adroit evasions of duty, he found himself obliged to work more than he found agreeable. He didn't see the fun of trudging after the deacon up and down the fields in the warm summer days. Even his meals did not yield unmingled satisfaction, as he had learned from experience that Mrs. Hopkins did not approve of giving him a second slice of pie, and in other cases interfered to check the complete gratification of his appetite, alleging that it wasn't good for boys to eat too much.

Sam took a different view of the matter, and felt that if he was willing to take the consequences, he ought to be allowed to eat as much as he pleased. He was not troubled with the catechism any more. The deacon found him so stolid and unteachable that he was forced to give up in despair, and Sam became master of his own time in the evening. He usually strayed into the village, where he found company at the village store. Here it was that he met a youth who was destined to exercise an important influence upon his career. This was Ben Barker, who had for a few months filled a position in a small retail store in New York city. Coming home, he found himself a great man. Country boys have generally a great curiosity about life in the great cities, and are eager to interview any one who can give them authentic details concerning it. For this reason Ben found himself much sought after by the village boys, and gave dazzling descriptions of life in the metropolis, about which he professed to be fully informed. Among his interested listeners was Sam, whose travels had been limited by a very narrow circle, but who, like the majority of boys, was possessed by a strong desire to see the world.

"I suppose there as many as a thousand houses in New York," he said to Ben.

"A thousand!" repeated Ben, in derision. "There's a million!"

"Honest?"

"Yes, they reach for miles and miles. There's about twenty thousand streets."

"It must be awfully big. I'd like to go there."

"Oh, you!" said Ben, contemptuously. "It wouldn't do for you to go there."

"Why not?"

"You couldn't get along nohow."

"I'd like to know why not?" said Sam, rather nettled at this depreciation.

"Oh, you're a country greenhorn. You'd get taken in right and left."

"I don't believe I would," said Sam. "I aint as green as you think."

"You'd better stay with the deacon, and hoe potatoes," said Ben, disparagingly. "It takes a smart fellow to succeed in New York."

"Is that the reason you had to come home?" retorted Sam.

"I'm going back pretty soon," said Ben. "I shan't stay long in such a one-horse place as this."

"Is it far to New York?" asked Sam, thoughtfully.

"Over a hundred miles."

"Does it cost much to go there?"

"Three dollars by the cars."

"That isn't so very much."

"No, but you've got to pay your expenses when you get there."

"I could work."

"What could you do? You might, perhaps, black boots in the City Hall Park."

"What pay do boys get for doing that?" asked Sam, seriously.

"Sometimes five cents, sometimes ten."

"I'd like it better than farmin!"

"It might do for you," said Ben, turning up his nose.

"What were you doing when you were in New York, Ben?"

"I was chief salesman in a dry goods store," said Ben, with an air of importance.

"Was it a good place?"

"Of course it was, or I wouldn't have stayed there."

"What made you leave it?"

"I had so much care and responsibility that the doctor told me I must have rest. When the boss was away, I run the store all alone."

There was no one to contradict Ben's confident assertions, and though some doubt was entertained by his listener none was expressed. Considering Ben's large claims, it was surprising that his services were not sought by leading New York firms, but, then, merit is not always appreciated at once. That was Ben's way of accounting for it.

Sam was never tired of asking Ben fresh questions about New York. His imagination had been inflamed by the glowing descriptions of the latter, and he was anxious to pass through a similar experience. In fact, he was slowly making up his mind to leave the deacon, and set out for the brilliant Paradise which so dazzled his youthful fancy. There was one drawback, however, and that a serious one, — the lack of funds. Though the deacon supplied him with board, and would doubtless keep him in wearing apparel, there was no hint or intimation of any further compensation for his services, and Sam's whole available money capital at this moment amounted to only three cents. Now three cents would purchase three sticks of candy, and Sam intended to appropriate them in this way, but they formed a slender fund for travelling expenses; and the worst of it was that Sam knew of no possible way of increasing them. If his journey depended upon that, it would be indefinitely postponed.

But circumstances favored his bold design, as we shall see.

One evening as Sam was returning from the store, a man from a neighboring town, who was driving by, reined up his horse, and said, "You live with Deacon Hopkins, don't you?"

"Yes, sir."

"Are you going home now?"

"Yes, sir."

"Then I'll hand you a note for him. Will you think to give it to him?"

"Yes, sir."

"I would stop myself, but I haven't time this evening."

"All right. I'll give it to him."

"Take good care of it, for there's money in it," said the man, as he passed it to the boy.

Money in it! This attracted Sam's attention, and excited his curiosity.

"I wonder how much there is in it," he thought to himself. "I wish it was mine. I could go to New York to-morrow if I only had it."

With this thought prominent in his mind, Sam entered the house. Mrs. Hopkins was at the table knitting, but the deacon was not to be seen.

"Where is the deacon?" asked Sam.

"He's gone to bed," said Mrs. Hopkins. "Did you want to see him?"

"No," said Sam, slowly.

"It's time you were abed too, Sam," said the lady. "You're out too late, as I was tellin' the deacon to-night. Boys like you ought to be abed at eight o'clock instead of settin' up half the night."

"I guess I'll go to bed now," said Sam, taking a lamp from the table.

"You'd better, and mind you get up early in the mornin'."

Sam did not answer, for he was busy thinking.

He went upstairs, fastened his door inside, and taking out the letter surveyed the outside critically. The envelope was not very securely fastened and came open. Sam could not resist the temptation presented, and drew out the inclosure. His face flushed with excitement, as he spread out two five-dollar bills on the table before him.

"Ten dollars!" ejaculated Sam. "What a lot of money! If it was only mine, I'd have enough to go to New York."

CHAPTER IX.

SAM TAKES FRENCH LEAVE.

If Sam had been brought up to entertain strict ideas on the subject of taking the property of others, and appropriating it to his own use, the temporary possession of the deacon's money would not have exposed him to temptation. But his conscience had never been awakened to the iniquity of theft. So when it occurred to him that he had in his possession money enough to gratify his secret desire, and carry him to New York, there to enter upon a brilliant career, it did not occur to him that it would be morally wrong to do so. He did realize the danger of detection, however, and balanced in his mind whether the risk was worth incurring. He decided that it was.

"The deacon don't know I've got the money," he reflected. "He won't find out for a good while;

when he does I shall be in New York, where he won't think of going to find me."

This was the way Sam reasoned, and from his point of view the scheme looked very plausible. Sam had a shrewd idea that his services were not sufficiently valuable to the deacon to induce him to make any extraordinary efforts for his capture. So, on the whole, he made up his mind to run away.

"Shall I go now, or wait till mornin'?" thought Sam.

He looked out of his window. There was no moon, and the night was therefore dark. It would not be very agreeable to roam about in the darkness. Besides, he was liable to lose his way. Again, he felt sleepy, and the bed looked very inviting.

"I'll wait till mornin'," thought Sam. "I'll start about four, and go over to Wendell, and take the train for New York. I'll be awful hungry when I get there. I wish I could wait till after breakfast; but it won't do."

Sam was not usually awake at four. Indeed he generally depended on being waked up by the deacon knocking on his door. But when boys or men have some pleasure in view it is apt to act upon the mind even when wrapped in slumber, and produce wakefulness. So Sam woke up about quarter of four. His plan flashed upon him, and he jumped out of bed. He dressed quickly, and, taking his shoes in his hand so that he might make no noise, he crept downstairs, and unlocked the front door, and then, after shutting it behind him, sat down on the front door-stone and put on his shoes.

"I guess they didn't hear me," he said to himself. "Now I'll be going."

The sun had not risen, but it was light with the gray light which precedes dawn. There was every promise of a fine day, and this helped to raise Sam's spirits.

"What'll the deacon say when he comes to wake me up?" thought our hero, though I am almost ashamed to give Sam such a name, for I am afraid he is acting in a manner very unlike the well-behaved heroes of most juvenile stories, my own among the number. However, since I have chosen to write about a "young outlaw," I must describe him as he is, and warn my boy readers that I by no means recommend them to pattern after him.

Before accompanying Sam on his travels, let us see how the deacon was affected by his flight.

At five o'clock he went up to Sam's door and knocked.

There was no answer.

The deacon knocked louder.

Still there was no answer.

"How sound the boy sleeps!" muttered the old man, and he applied his knuckles vigorously to the door. Still without effect. Thereupon he tried the door, and found that it was unlocked. He opened it, and walked to the bed, not doubting that he would see Sam fast asleep. But a surprise awaited him. The bed was empty, though it had evidently been occupied during the night.

"Bless my soul! the boy's up," ejaculated the deacon.

A wild idea came to him that Sam had voluntarily got up at this early hour, and gone to work, but he dismissed it at once as absurd. He knew Sam far too well for that.

Why, then, had he got up? Perhaps he was unwell, and could not sleep. Not dreaming of his running away, this seemed to the deacon the most plausible way of accounting for Sam's disappearance, but he decided to go down and communicate the news to his wife.

"Why were you gone so long, deacon?" asked Mrs. Hopkins. "Couldn't you wake him up?"

"He wasn't there."

"Wasn't where?"

"In bed."

"What do you mean?"

"I mean that Sam's got up already. I couldn't find him."

"Couldn't find him?"

"No, Martha."

"Had the bed been slept in?"

"Of course. I s'pose he was sick, and couldn't sleep, so he went downstairs."

"Perhaps he's gone down to the pantry," said Mrs. Hopkins, suspiciously. "I'll go down and see."

She went downstairs, followed by the deacon. She instituted an examination, but found Sam guiltless of a fresh attempt upon the provision department. She went to the front door, and found it unlocked.

"He's gone out," she said.

"So he has, but I guess he'll be back to breakfast," said the deacon.

"I don't," said the lady.

"Why not?"

"Because I think he's run away."

"Run away!" exclaimed the deacon. "Why, I never had a boy run away from me."

"Well, you have now."

"Where would he go? He aint no home. He wouldn't go to the poorhouse."

"Of course not. I never heard of anybody that had a comfortable home running away to the poorhouse."

"But why should he run away?" argued the deacon.

"Boys often run away," said his wife, sententiously.

"He had no cause."

"Yes, he had. You made him work, and he's lazy, and don't like work. I'm not surprised at all."

"I s'pose I'd better go after him," said the deacon.

"Don't you stir a step to go, deacon. He aint worth going after. I'm glad we've got rid of him."

"Well, he didn't do much work," admitted the deacon.

"While he ate enough for two boys. Good riddance to bad rubbish, I say."

"I don't know how he's goin' to get along. He didn't have no money."

"I don't care how he gets along, as long as he don't come back. There's plenty of better boys you can get."

Sam would not have felt flattered, if he had heard this final verdict upon his merits. It must be confessed, however, that it was well deserved.

A few days afterwards, the deacon obtained the services of another boy, whom he found more satisfactory than the runaway, and Sam was no longer missed. It was not till the tenth day that he learned of the theft. While riding on that day, he met Mr. Comstock, who had confided to Sam the money-letter.

"Good-morning, Deacon Hopkins," said he, stopping his horse.

"Good-morning," said the deacon.

"I suppose your boy handed you a letter from me."

"I haven't received any letter," said the deacon, surprised.

"It was early last week that I met a boy who said he lived with you. As I was in a hurry, I gave him a letter containing ten dollars, which I asked him to give to you."

"What day was it?" asked the deacon, eagerly.

"Monday. Do you mean to say he didn't give it to you?"

"No; he ran away the next morning, and I haven't seen him since."

"Then he ran away with the money — the young thief! I told him there was money in it."

"Bless my soul! I didn't think Sam was so bad," ejaculated the deacon.

"Didn't you go after him?"

"No; he wasn't very good to work, and I thought I'd let him run. Ef I'd knowed about the money, I'd have gone after him."

"It isn't too late, now."

"I'll ask my wife what I'd better do."

The deacon conferred with his wife, who was greatly incensed against Sam, and would have advised pursuit, but they had no clue to his present whereabouts.

"He'll come back some time, deacon," said she. "When he does, have him took up."

But years passed, and Sam did not come back, nor did the deacon set eyes on him for four years, and then under the circumstances recorded in the first chapter.

CHAPTER X.

SAM'S ADVENTURES AT THE DEPOT.

It was six miles to the station at Wendell, where Sam proposed to take the cars for New York. He had to travel on an empty stomach, and naturally got ravenously hungry before he reached his destination. About half a mile this side of the depot he passed a grocery-store, and it occurred to him that he might get something to eat there.

Entering he saw a young man in his shirt-sleeves engaged in sweeping.

"Have you got anything good to eat?" asked Sam.

"This aint a hotel," said the young man, taking Sam for a penniless adventurer.

"I knew that before," said Sam, "but haven't you got some crackers or something, to stay a feller's stomach?"

"Haven't you had any breakfast?" asked the clerk, curiously.

"No."

"Don't they give you breakfast where you live?"

"Not so early in the morning. You see I had to take an early start, 'cause I'm goin' to attend my grandmother's funeral."

This of course was a story trumped up for the occasion.

"We've got some raw potatoes," said the clerk, grinning.

"I've had enough to do with potatoes," said Sam. "Haven't you got some crackers?"

"Come to think of it, we have. How many will you have?"

"About a dozen."

While they were being put up in a paper bag, the clerk inquired, "How far off does your grandmother live?"

"About twenty miles from here, on the railroad," answered Sam, who did'nt care to mention that he was bound for New York.

"Warwick, I suppose."

"Yes," said Sam, at a venture. "How soon does the train start?"

"In about half an hour. Hold on, though; that's the New York train, and don't stop at Warwick."

"I guess I'll be goin'," said Sam, hurriedly. "Where's the depot?"

"Half a mile straight ahead, but you needn't hurry. The train for Warwick don't go till ten."

"Never mind. I want to see the New York train start;" and Sam hurried off eating crackers as he walked.

"I'm glad the train starts so quick," thought Sam. "I don't want to wait round here long. I might meet somebody that knows me."

He had no difficulty in finding the depot. It was a plain building, about twenty by thirty feet, with a piazza on the side towards the track. He entered, and going up to the ticket-office asked for a ticket to New York.

"For yourself?" asked the station-master.

"Yes," said Sam.

"How old are you?"

"Twelve."

"Then you'll have to pay for a whole ticket. Three dollars."

"All right," said Sam, promptly, and he drew out a five-dollar bill, receiving in return two dollars and a ticket.

"Do you live in New York, sonny?" asked the station-master.

"No, I'm only goin' to see my aunt," answered Sam, with another impromptu falsehood.

"I know something about New York. In what street does your aunt live?"

Sam was posed, for he did not know the name of even one street in the city he was going to.

"I don't exactly remember," he was forced to admit.

"Then how do you expect to find her if you don't know where she lives?"

"Oh, she'll meet me at the depot," said Sam, readily.

"Suppose she don't?"

"I'll find her somehow. But she's sure to meet me."

"Going to stay long in the city?"

"I hope so. Perhaps my aunt'll adopt me. How soon will the train be along?"

"In about fifteen minutes."

Here an old lady came up, and asked for a ticket to New York.

"Three dollars, ma'am."

"Three dollars! Can't you take less?" asked the old lady, fumbling in her pocket for her purse.

"No ma'am, the price is fixed."

"It's a sight of money. Seems throwed away, too, jest for travellin'. You haint got anything to show for it. I never was to York in my life."

"Please hurry, ma'am, there are others waiting."

"Massy sakes, don't be so hasty! There's the money."

"And there's your ticket."

"I wish I know'd somebody goin' to New York. I'm afeared to travel alone."

"There's a boy going," said the station-master, pointing to Sam.

"Are you goin' to York?" asked the old lady, peering over her spectacles at Sam.

"Yes, ma'am."

"Was you ever there afore?"

"No, ma'am."

"Aint your folks afeared to have you go alone?"

"Oh, no, they don't mind."

"I wish you was older, so's you could look after me."

Sam was rather flattered by the idea of having a lady under his charge, and said, "I'll take care of you, if you want me to."

"Will you? That's a good boy. What's your name?"

"Sam Barker," answered our hero, with some hesitation, not feeling sure whether it was politic to mention his real name.

"Do you live in New York?"

"No, ma'am; but I'm goin' to."

"When will the cars git along?"

"In about ten minutes."

"You'll help me get in, won't you? I've got two bandboxes, and I don't know how to manage."

"Yes, ma'am, I'll help you. I'm goin' out on the platform, but I'll come in when the cars come along."

Sam went out on the platform, and watched eagerly for the approach of the cars. Up they came, thundering along the track, and Sam rushed into the depot in excitement.

"Come along, ma'am," he said. "The cars are here."

The old lady was in a flutter of excitement also. She seized one bandbox, and Sam the other, and they hurried out on the platform. They were just climbing up the steps, when the conductor asked, "Where are you going?"

"To York, of course."

"Then this isn't the train. It is going in the opposite direction."

"Lawful suz!" ejaculated the old lady in dismay. "What made you tell me wrong, you bad boy?" and she glared at him reproachfully over her glasses.

"How should I know?" said Sam, rather abashed. "I didn't know about no other train."

"You come near makin' me go wrong."

"I can't help it. It would be just as bad for me."

"When does the train go to York, somebody?" asked the old lady, looking about her in a general way.

"Next train; comes round in about five minutes."

Sam helped the old lady back into the depot, rather ashamed of the mistake he had made. He saw that she had lost some of her confidence in him, and it mortified him somewhat.

It was nearly ten minutes afterwards, — for the train was late, — before the right cars came up.

Sam dashed into the depot again, and seized a bandbox.

"Here's the cars. Come along," he said.

"I won't stir a step till I know if it's the right cars," said the old lady firmly.

"Then you may stay here," said Sam. "I'm goin'."

"Don't leave your grandmother," said a gentleman, standing by.

"She isn't my grandmother. Isn't this the train to New York?"

"Yes."

Sam seized the bandbox once more, and this time the old lady followed him.

They got into the cars without difficulty, and the old lady breathed a sigh of relief.

Sam took a seat at the window just behind her, and

his heart bounded with exultation as he reflected that in a few hours he would be in the great city, of which he had such vague and wonderful ideas. The only drawback to his enjoyment was the loss of his usual morning meal. The crackers helped to fill him up, but they were a poor substitute for the warm breakfast to which he had been accustomed at the deacon's. Still Sam did not wish himself back. Indeed, as he thought of the deacon's bewilderment on discovering his disappearance, he broke into an involuntary laugh.

"What are you laffin' at?" asked the old lady, suspiciously.

Sam answered, "I was thinkin' how near we came to bein' carried off to the wrong place."

"That ain't anything to laff at," said the old lady, grimly.

CHAPTER XI.

FIRST EXPERIENCES IN THE CITY.

THERE are few boys who do not enjoy a trip on the railroad, especially for the first time. The five hours which Sam spent on his journey gave him unqualified delight. Occasionally his attention was called off from the scenery by an exclamation from the old lady, who at every jolt thought the cars were off the track.

Sam liberally patronized the apple and peanut merchant, who about once an hour walked through the cars. The crackers which he had purchased at the grocery store had not spoiled his appetite, but rather appeared to sharpen it. The old lady apparently became hungry also, for she called the apple vender to her.

"What do you ask for them apples?" she inquired.

"The largest are three cents apiece, the smallest, two cents."

"That's an awful price. They aint worth half that."

"We can't sell 'em for less, and make any profit."

"I'll give you a cent for that one," she continued, pointing to the largest in the basket.

"That! Why, that's a three-center. Can't take it nohow."

"I'll give you three cents for them two."

"No, ma'am, you may have 'em for five cents."

"Then I won't buy 'em. My darter will give me plenty for nothin'."

"She may, but I can't."

So the old lady heroically put away the temptation, and refused to purchase.

All things must have an end, and Sam's journey was at length over. The cars entered the great depot. Sam hurried out of the cars, never giving a thought to the old lady, who expected his help in carrying out her bandboxes. He was eager to make his first acquaintance with the streets of New York. There was a crowd of hackmen in waiting, all of whom appeared to Sam to be seeing which could talk fastest.

"Have a carriage, sir? Take you to any hotel."

One of them got hold of Sam by the arms, and attempted to lead him to his carriage.

"Hold on a minute, mister," said Sam, drawing back. "Where are you goin' to take me?"

"Anywhere you say. Astor House, St. Nicholas, or any other."

"Is it far?"

"About five miles," said the hackman, glibly.

"How much are you goin' to charge?"

"Only three dollars."

"Three dollars!" repeated Sam, in amazement.

He had less than seven dollars now, and, though he was not particularly provident, he knew that it would never do to spend almost half his slender stock of money for cab-hire.

"Never mind," said he. "I'll walk."

"You can't; it's too far," said the hackman, eager for a fare.

"I'll try."

So Sam walked out of the depot, and walked away. He didn't know exactly where to go, and thought he would follow a man with a carpet-bag who appeared to know his way. This man unconsciously guided him to Broadway. Sam realized, from the stately character of the buildings, that he was in an important street, and, cutting loose from his guide, walked down towards the City Hall Park. It seemed to him like a dream; these beautiful warehouses, showy stores, and the moving throng, which never seemed to grow less, surprised him also. Though he knew in advance that New York must be very different from the little country town which, until now, had been his home, he was not prepared for so great a difference, and wandered on, his mouth and eyes wide open.

At last he reached the City Hall Park, and, catching sight of a bench on which one or two persons were already sitting, Sam, feeling tired with his walk, entered the Park, and sat down too.

"Black yer boots?" inquired a dirty-faced boy, with a box slung over his shoulders.

Sam looked at his shoes, begrimed with a long country walk, and hesitated.

"What do you ask?" he said.

"It's worth a quarter to black them shoes," said the boy, swinging them critically.

"Then I can't afford it."

"Twenty cents."

"No," said Sam. "I've got to earn my own living, and I can't afford it. Is blackin' boots a good business?"

"Some days it is, but if it comes rainy, it isn't. I'll give you a bully shine for ten cents."

"Will you show me afterwards where I can get some dinner cheap?" asked Sam, who was still hungry.

"Yes," said the boot-black. "I know a tip-top place."

"Is it far off?"

"Right round in Chatham street — only a minute's walk."

"All right. Go ahead. I'll give you ten cents."

Sam felt that he was paying his money not only for the actual service done, but for valuable information besides. On the whole, though he knew he must be economical, it seemed to him a paying investment.

"Did you come from the country?" asked the

young knight of the blacking-brush, while he was vigorously brushing the first shoe.

"Yes," said Sam. "I only got here just now."

"That's what I thought."

"Why?"

"Because you look like a greenhorn."

"Do you mean to insult me?" asked Sam, nettled.

"No," said the other; "only if you've never been here before of course you're green."

"I won't be long," said Sam, hastily.

"Course you won't, 'specially if you have me to show you round."

"Have you lived long in New York?" inquired Sam.

"I was born here," said the boy.

"Have you been long blackin' boots?"

"Ever since I was knee-high to a door-step."

"Then you make a living at it?"

"I don't starve. What made you leave the country?"

"I got tired of working on a farm."

"Did you have enough to eat?"

"Yes."

"And a good bed to sleep in?"

"Yes."

"Then you'd ought to have stayed there," said the boot-black.

"I think I shall like the city better," said Sam. "There's a good deal more goin' on."

"I'd like to try the country. You don't live at the West, do you?"

"No."

"Lots of boys goes West. Maybe I'll go there, some time."

"Is it a good place?"

"That's what they say. The boys gets good homes out there on farms."

"Then I don't want to go," said Sam. "I'm tired of farmin'."

By this time the shoes were polished.

"Aint that a bully shine?" asked the boot-black, surveying his work with satisfaction.

"Yes," said Sam. "You know how to do it."

"Course I do. Now where's the stamps?"

Sam drew out ten cents, and handed to the boy.

"Now show me where I can get some dinner."

"All right. Come along!" and the boy, slinging his box over his shoulder, led the way to a small place on Chatham street. It was in a basement, and did not look over-neat; but Sam was too hungry to be particular, and the odor of the cooking was very grateful to him.

"I guess I'll get a plate o' meat, too," said the boot-black. "I aint had anything since breakfast."

They sat down side by side at a table, and Sam looked over the bill of fare. He finally ordered a plate of roast beef, for ten cents, and his companion followed his example. The plates were brought, accompanied by a triangular wedge of bread, and a small amount of mashed potato. It was not a feast for an epicure, but both Sam and his companion appeared to enjoy it.

Sam was still hungry.

"They didn't bring much," he said. "I guess I'll have another plate."

"I aint got stamps enough," said his companion.

"If you want another plate, I'll pay for it," said Sam, with a sudden impulse of generosity.

"Will you? You're a brick!" said the bootblack heartily. "Then I don't mind. I'll have another."

"Do they have any pie?" asked Sam.

"Course they do."

"Then I'll have a piece afterwards."

He did not offer to treat his companion to pie, for he realized that his stock of money was not inexhaustible. This did not appear to be expected, however, and the two parted on very good terms, when the dinner was over.

CHAPTER XII.

CLARENCE BROWN.

SAM continued to walk about in the neighborhood of the City Hall Park, first in one direction, then in another; but at last he became fatigued. It had been an unusually exciting day, and he had taken more exercise than usual, though he had not worked; for his morning walk, added to his rambles about the city streets, probably amounted to not less than twelve miles. Then, too, Sam began to realize what older and more extensive travellers know well, that nothing is more wearisome than sight-seeing.

So the problem forced itself upon his attention — where was he to sleep? The bed he slept in the night before was more than a hundred miles away. It struck Sam as strange, for we must remember how inexperienced he was, that he must pay for the use of a bed. How much, he had no idea, but felt that it was time to make some inquiries.

He went into a hotel on the European system, and asked a man who was standing at the cigar stand, "What do you charge for sleeping here?"

"Ask of that man at the desk," said the cigar-vender.

Sam followed directions, and, approaching the room-clerk, preferred the same inquiry.

"One dollar," was the answer.

"One dollar, just for sleeping?" inquired Sam, in surprise, for in his native village he knew that the school-teacher got boarded for three dollars a week, board and lodging complete for seven days.

"Those are our terms," said the clerk.

"I don't care about a nice room," said Sam, hoping to secure a reduction.

"We charge more for our nice rooms," said the clerk.

"Aint there any cheaper hotels?" asked our hero, rather dismayed at his sudden discovery of the great cost of living in New York.

"I suppose so," said the clerk, carelessly; but he did not volunteer any information as to their whereabouts.

Sam walked slowly out of the hotel, quite uncertain where to go, or what to do. He had money enough to pay for a night's lodging, even at this high price, but he judged wisely that he could not afford to spend so large a part of his small stock of money.

"I wondor where the boys sleep that black boots," he thought. "They can't pay a dollar a night for sleeping."

He looked around for the boy who had guided him to a restaurant, but could not find him.

It was now eight o'clock, and he begun to think he should have to go back to the hotel after all, when a shabby-looking man, with watery eyes and a red nose, accosted him.

"Are you a stranger in the city, my young friend?" he asked.

"Yes," said Sam, rather relieved at the opportunity of speaking to somebody.

"So I thought. Where are you boarding?"

"Nowhere," said Sam.

"Where do you sleep to-night?"

"I don't know," said Sam, rather helplessly.

"Why don't you go to a hotel?"

"They charge too much," said Sam.

"Haven't you got money enough to pay for a lodging at a hotel?" asked the stranger, with rather less interest in his manner.

"Oh, yes," said Sam, "a good deal more than that; but then, I want to make my money last till I can earn something."

"To be sure, to be sure," answered the stranger, his interest returning. "You are quite right, my dear friend. I am glad to see that you are so sensible. Of course you ought not to go to a hotel. They charge too high altogether."

"But I must sleep somewhere," said Sam, anxiously. "I only got to New York this morning, and I don't know where to go."

"Of course, of course. I thought you might be in trouble, seeing you were a stranger. It's lucky you met me."

"Can you tell me of any place to spend the night?" asked Sam, encouraged by the stranger's manner.

"Yes; I'll let you stay with me, and it shan't cost you a cent."

"Thank you," said Sam, congratulating himself on his good luck in meeting so benevolent a man. He could not help admitting to himself that the philanthropist looked shabby, even seedy. He was not the sort of man from whom he would have expected such kindness, but that made no difference. The offer was evidently a desirable one, and Sam accepted it without a moment's hesitation.

"I remember when I came to the city myself," explained the stranger. "I was worse off than you, for I had no money at all. A kind man gave me a night's lodging, just as I offer one to you, and I determined that I would do the same by others when I had a chance."

"You are very kind," said Sam.

"Perhaps you won't say so when you see my room," said the other. "I am not a rich man.'

Glancing at the man's attire, Sam found no difficulty in believing him. Our hero, though not very observing, was not prepossessed in favor of the New York tailors by what he saw, for the stranger's coat was very long, while his pants were very short, and his vest was considerably too large for him. Instead of a collar and cravat, he wore a ragged silk handkerchief tied round his throat. His hat was crumpled and greasy, and the best that could be said of it was, that it corresponded with the rest of his dress.

"I don't live in a very nice place," said the stranger; "but perhaps you can put up with it for one night."

"Oh, I don't mind," said Sam, hastily. "I aint used to anything very nice."

"Then it's all right," said the stranger. "Such as it is, you are welcome. Now, I suppose you are tired."

"Yes, I am," said Sam.

"Then I'll take you to my room at once. We'll go up Centre street."

Sam cheerfully followed his conductor. He felt like a storm-tossed mariner, who has just found port.

"What is your name?" asked his guide.

"Sam Barker."

"Mine is Clarence Brown."

"Is it?" asked Sam.

He could not help thinking the name too fine for a man of such shabby appearance, and yet it would be hard, when names are so cheap, if all the best ones should be bestowed on the wealthy.

"It's a good name, isn't it?" asked the stranger.

"Tip-top."

"I belong to a good family, though you wouldn't think it to look at me now," continued his guide. "My father was a wealthy merchant."

"Was he?" asked Sam, curiously.

"Yes, we lived in a splendid mansion, and kept plenty of servants. I was sent to an expensive school, and I did not dream of coming to this."

Mr. Brown wiped his eyes with his coat-sleeve, as he thus revived the memories of his early opulence.

"Did your father lose his money?" asked Sam, getting interested.

"He did indeed," said the stranger, with emotion. "It was in the panic of 1837. Did you ever hear of it?"

"I guess not," said Sam, who was not very conversant with the financial history of the country.

"My father became a bankrupt, and soon after died of grief," continued the stranger. "I was called back from boarding-school, and thrown upon the cold mercies of the world."

"That was hard on you," said Sam.

"It was, indeed, my young friend. I perceive that you have a sympathetic heart. You can feel for the woes of others."

"Yes," said Sam, concluding that such an answer was expected.

"I am glad I befriended you. Have you also seen better days?"

"Well, I don't know," said Sam. "It's been pleasant enough to-day."

"I don't mean that. I mean, were you ever rich?"

"Not that I can remember," said Sam.

"Then you don't know what it is to be reduced from affluence to poverty. It is a bitter experience."

"I should think so," said Sam, who felt a little tired of Clarence Brown's reminiscences, and wondered how soon they would reach that gentleman's house.

Meanwhile they had gone up Centre street, and turned into Leonard street. It was not an attractive locality, nor were the odors that reached Sam's nose very savory.

"This is where I live," said Mr. Brown, pausing before a large and dilapidated-looking tenement house of discolored brick.

"You don't live here alone, do you?" inquired Sam, who was not used to crowded tenement houses.

"Oh, no, I only occupy an humble room up-stairs. Follow me, and I'll lead you to it."

The staircase was dirty, and in keeping with the external appearance of the house. The wall paper was torn off in places, and contrasted very unfavorably with the neat house of Deacon Hopkins. Sam noticed this, but he was tired and sleepy, and was not disposed to be over-critical, as he followed Mr. Brown in silence to the fourth floor.

CHAPTER XIII.

ROBBED IN HIS SLEEP.

Arrived at his destination Mr. Brown opened a door, and bade Sam enter. It was rather dark, and it was not until his host lighted a candle, that Sam could obtain an idea of the appearance of the room. The ceiling was low, and the furniture scanty. A couple of chairs, a small table, of which the paint was worn off in spots, and a bed in the corner, were the complete outfit of Mr. Brown's home. He set the candle on the table, and remarked apologetically: "I don't live in much style, as you see. The fact is, I am at present in straitened circumstances. When my uncle dies I shall inherit a fortune. Then, when you come to see me, I will entertain you handsomely."

"Is your uncle rich?" asked Sam.

"I should say he was. He's a millionnaire."

"Why don't he do something for you now?"

Mr. Clarence Brown shrugged his shoulders.

"He's a very peculiar man — wants to keep every cent as long as he lives. When he's dead it's got to go to his heirs. That's why he lives in a palatial mansion on Madison Avenue, while I, his nephew, occupy a shabby apartment like this."

Sam looked about him, and mentally admitted the justice of the term. It was a shabby apartment, without question. Still, he was to lodge there gratis, and it was not for him to complain.

"By the way," said Mr. Brown, casually, after exploring his pockets apparently without success, "you haven't got a quarter, have you?"

"Yes, I guess so."

"All right; I'll borrow it till to-morrow, if you don't mind."

"Certainly," said Sam, handing over the sum desired.

"I'll go out and get some whiskey. My system requires it. You won't mind being left alone for five minutes."

"Oh, no."

"Very good. I won't stay long."

Mr. Brown went out, and our hero sat down on the bed to wait for him.

"So this is my first night in the city," he thought. "I expected they had better houses.. This room isn't half so nice as I had at the deacon's. But then I haven't got to hoe potatoes. I guess I'll like it when I get used to it. There isn't anybody to order me round here."

Presently Mr. Brown came back. He had a bottle partially full of whiskey with him.

"Sorry to keep you waiting," he said. "Were you lonely?"

"Oh, no."

"I've got a couple of glasses here somewhere. Oh, here they are. Now we'll see how it tastes."

"Not much for me," said Sam. "I don't think I'll like it."

"It'll be good for your stomach. However, I won't give you much."

He poured out a little in one tumbler for Sam, and a considerably larger amount for himself.

"Your health," he said, nodding.

"Thank you," said Sam.

Sam tasted the whiskey, but the taste did not please him. He set down the glass, but his host drained his at a draught.

"Don't you like it?" asked Brown.

"Not very much."

"Don't you care to drink it?"

"I guess not."

"It's a pity it should be wasted."

To prevent this, Mr. Brown emptied Sam's glass also.

"Now, if you are not sleepy, we might have a game of cards," suggested Brown.

"I think I'd rather go to bed," said Sam, yawning.

"All right! Go to bed any time. I dare say you are tired. Do you go to sleep easily?"

"In a jiffy."

"Then you won't mind my absence. I've got to make a call on a sick friend, but I shan't be out late. Just make yourself at home, go to sleep, and you'll see me in the morning."

"Thank you, sir."

"Don't bolt the door, as I don't want to wake you up when I come in."

"All right."

Again Mr. Brown went out, and Sam undressed and got into bed. It was not very comfortable, and the solitary sheet looked as if it had not been changed for three months or more. However, Sam was not fastidious, and he was sleepy. So he closed his eyes, and was soon in the land of dreams.

It was about two hours afterward that Clarence Brown entered the room. He walked on tiptoe to the bed, and looked at Sam.

"He's fast asleep," he said to himself. "Did he undress? Oh, yes, here are his clothes. I'll take the liberty of examining his pockets, to see whether my trouble is likely to be rewarded."

Brown explored one pocket after the other. He found no pocket-book, for Sam did not possess any. In fact he had never felt the need of one until he appropriated the deacon's money. The balance of this was tucked away in his vest-pocket.

"Six dollars and ten cents," said Brown, after counting it. "It isn't much of a haul, that's a fact. I thought he had twice as much, at the least. Still," he added philosophically, "it's better than nothing. I shall find a use for it without doubt."

He tucked the money away in his own pocket, and sat on the edge of the bedstead in meditation.

"I may as well go to bed," he reflected. "He won't find out his loss in the night, and in the morning I can be off before he is up. Even if I oversleep myself, I can brazen it out. He's only a green country boy. Probably he won't suspect me, and if he does he can prove nothing."

He did not undress, but lay down on the bed dressed as he was. He, too, was soon asleep, and Sam, unconscious of his loss, slept on. So the money was doubly stolen, and the first thief suffered at the hands of a more experienced thief.

The sun had been up nearly three hours the next morning before Clarence Brown awoke. As he opened his eyes, his glance fell on Sam still asleep, and the events of the evening previous came to his mind.

"I must be up, and out of this," he thought, "before the young greenhorn wakes up."

Being already dressed, with the exception of his

coat, he had little to do beyond rising. He crept out of the room on tiptoe, and, making his way to a restaurant at a safe distance, sat down and ordered a good breakfast at Sam's expense.

Meanwhile Sam slept on for half an hour more.

Finally he opened his eyes, and, oblivious of his changed circumstances, was surprised that he had not been called earlier. But a single glance about the shabby room recalled to his memory that he was now beyond the deacon's jurisdiction.

"I am in New York," he reflected, with a thrill of joy. "But where is Mr. Brown?"

He looked in vain for his companion, but no suspicion was excited in his mind.

"He didn't want to wake me up," he thought. "I suppose he has gone to his business."

He stretched himself, and lay a little longer. It was a pleasant thought that there was no stern taskmaster to force him up. He might lie as long as he wanted to, — till noon, if he chose. Perhaps he might have chosen, but the claims of a healthy appetite asserted themselves, and Sam sprang out of bed.

"I'll have a good breakfast," he said to himself,

"and then I must look around and see if I can't find something to do; my money will soon be out."

It was natural that he should have felt for his money, at that moment, but he did not. No suspicion of Mr. Brown's integrity had entered his mind. You see Sam was very unsophisticated at that time, and, though he had himself committed a theft, he did not suspect the honesty of others.

"I suppose I shall have to go without thanking Mr. Brown, as he don't seem to be here," he reflected. "Perhaps I shall see him somewhere about the streets. I've saved a dollar anyway, or at least seventy-five cents," he added, thinking of the quarter he had lent his hospitable entertainer the evening before. "Perhaps he'll let me sleep here again to-night. It'll be a help to me, as long as I haven't got anything to do yet."

Still Sam did not feel for his money, and was happily unconscious of his loss.

He opened his door, and found his way downstairs into the street without difficulty. The halls and staircases looked even more dingy and shabby in the daytime than they had done in the evening. "It isn't a very nice place to live," thought Sam. "However, I suppose Mr. Brown will be rich when his uncle dies. I wish he was rich now; he might give me a place."

"Shine yer boots?" asked a small knight of the brush.

"No," said Sam, who had grown economical; "they don't need it."

He walked on for five minutes or more. Presently he came to an eating-house. He knew it by the printed bills of fare which were placarded outside.

"Now, I'll have some breakfast," he thought, with satisfaction, and he entered confidently.

CHAPTER XIV.

BOUNCED!

SAM sat down at a table, and took up the bill of fare. A colored waiter stood by, and awaited his orders.

"Bring me a plate of beefsteak, a cup of coffee, and some tea-biscuit," said Sam, with the air of a man of fortune.

"All right, sir," said the waiter.

"After all, it's pleasant living in New York," thought Sam, as he leaned back in his chair, and awaited in pleasant anticipation the fulfilment of his order. "It's different from livin' at the deacon's. Here a feller can be independent."

"As long as he has money," Sam should have added; but, like some business men, he was not aware of his present insolvency. Ignorance is bliss, sometimes; and it is doubtful whether our hero would have eaten his breakfast with as good a relish when it came, if he had known that he had not a cent in his pocket.

Sam was soon served, and he soon made way with the articles he had ordered. You can't get a very liberal supply of beefsteak for fifteen cents, which was what Sam was charged for his meat. He felt hungry still, after he had eaten what was set before him. So he took the bill of fare once more, and pored over its well-filled columns.

"They must have a tremendous big kitchen to cook so many things," he thought. "Why, there are as many as a hundred. Let me see — here's buckwheat cakes, ten cents. I guess I'll have some."

"Anything more, sir?" asked the waiter, approaching to clear away the dirty dishes.

"Buckwheat cakes, and another cup of coffee," ordered Sam.

"All right, sir."

"They treat me respectful, here," thought Sam. "What would the deacon say to hear me called sir? I like it. Folks have better manners in the city than in the country."

This was rather a hasty conclusion on the part of

Sam, and it was not long before he had occasion enough to change his mind.

He ate the buckwheat cakes with a relish, and felt tolerably satisfied.

"Anything more, sir?" asked the waiter.

Sam was about to say no, when his eye rested on that portion of the bill devoted to pastry, and he changed his mind.

"Bring me a piece of mince-pie," he said.

Sam was sensible that he was ordering breakfast beyond his means, but he vaguely resolved that he would content himself with a small dinner. He really could not resist the temptation of the pie.

At last it was eaten, and the waiter brought him a ticket, bearing the price of his breakfast, fifty cents. Now, for the first time, he felt in his vest-pocket for his money. He felt in vain. Still he did not suspect his loss.

"I thought I put it in my vest-pocket," he said to himself. "I guess I made a mistake, and put it in some other."

He felt in another pocket, and still another, till

he had explored every pocket he possessed, and still no money.

Sam turned pale, and his heart gave a sudden thump, as the extent of his misfortune dawned upon him. It was not alone that he was without money in a strange city, but he had eaten rather a hearty breakfast, which he was unable to pay for. What would they think of him? What would they do to him? He saw it all now. That specious stranger, Clarence Brown, had robbed him in his sleep. That was why he had invited him to spend the night in his room without charge. That was why he had got up so early and stolen out without his knowledge, after he had purloined all his money.

Sam was not particularly bashful; but he certainly felt something like it, as he walked up to the cashier's desk. A man stood behind it, rather stout, and on the whole not benevolent in his looks. There was no softness about his keen business face. Sam inferred with a sinking heart that he was not a man likely to sympathize with him in his misfortunes, or seem to give credence to them.

Sam stood at the counter waiting while the proprietor was making change for another customer. He was considering what he could best say to propitiate his creditor.

"Now, then," said the man behind the counter, a little impatiently, for another had come up behind Sam, "where's your ticket?"

"Here, sir," said Sam, laying it on the counter.

"Fifty cents. Pay quick, and don't keep me waiting."

"I am very sorry, sir," Sam began, faltering, "but—"

"But what!" exclaimed the proprietor, with an ominous scowl.

"I can't pay you now."

"Can't pay me now!" repeated the other, angrily; "what do you mean?"

"I've lost my money," said Sam, feeling more and more uncomfortable.

By this time the patience of the restaurant-keeper was quite gone.

"What business had you to come in here and order an expensive breakfast when you had no money?" he demanded, furiously.

"I thought I had some money," said Sam, fervently wishing himself back at the deacon's for the first time since his arrival in the city.

"How could you think you had some when you hadn't any?"

"I had some last night," said Sam, eagerly; "but I slept in Mr. Brown's room, and he must have robbed me in the night."

"That's a likely story!" sneered the proprietor. "What do you think of it, Mr. Jones?" he asked, turning to a customer, whom he knew by name.

Mr. Jones shrugged his shoulders.

"Too thin!" he replied, briefly.

"Of course it is," said the proprietor, angrily. "This boy's evidently a beat."

"A what?" inquired Sam, who had not been in the city long enough to understand the meaning of the term.

"A dead beat; but you don't play any of your games on me, young man. I've cut my eye-teeth, I have. You don't swindle me out of a fifty-cent breakfast quite so easily. Here, John, call a policeman."

"Oh, don't call a policeman!" exclaimed Sam, terror-stricken. "It's true, every word I've told you. I'm from the country. I only got to the city yesterday, and I've been robbed of all my money, over six dollars. I hope you'll believe me."

"I don't believe a word you say," said the restaurant-keeper, harshly. "You are trying to come it over me. I dare say you've been round the streets half your life."

"I think you are wrong, Mr. Chucks," said another customer, who was waiting to pay his bill. "He's got a country look about him. He don't look like one of the regular street boys. Better let him go. I wouldn't call a policeman."

"I ought to," grumbled the proprietor. "Fancy his impudence in ordering a fifty-cent breakfast, when he hadn't a cent to pay his bill."

"I wouldn't have come in, if I had known," said Sam.

"Don't tell me," said the man, sharply, "for I don't believe it. Do you think I can afford to give you breakfast for nothing?"

"I'll pay you as soon as I get some money," said Sam. "Only don't send me to prison."

"I won't give you in charge this time, though I ought to; but I'll give you something to settle your breakfast. Here, Peter, you waited on this young man, didn't you?"

"Yes, sir."

"He hasn't paid for his breakfast, and pretends he hasn't got any money. *Bounce him!*"

If Sam was ignorant of the meaning of the word "bounce," he was soon enlightened. The waiter seized him by the collar, before he knew what was going to happen, pushed him to the door, and then, lifting his foot by a well-directed kick, landed him across the sidewalk into the street.

This proceeding was followed by derisive laughter from the other waiters who had gathered near the door, and it was echoed by two street urchins outside, who witnessed Sam's ignominous exit from the restaurant.

Sam staggered from the force of the bouncing, and felt disgraced and humiliated to think that the waiter who had been so respectful and attentive should have inflicted upon him such an indignity, which he had no power to resent.

"I wish I was back at the deacon's," he thought bitterly.

"How do you feel?" asked one of the boys who had witnessed Sam's humiliation, not sympathetically, but in a tone of mockery.

"None of your business!" retorted Sam, savagely.

"He feels bad, Mickey," said the other. "He's heard bad news, and that's what made him in such a hurry."

Here both the boys laughed, and Sam retorted angrily, "I'll make you feel bad, if you aint careful."

"Hear him talk, Mickey, — aint he smart?"

"I'll make you both smart," said Sam, beginning to roll up his sleeves; for he was no coward, and the boys were only about his own size.

"He wants to bounce us, like he was bounced himself," said Pat Riley. "How did it feel, Johnny?"

Sam gave chase, but his tormentors were better acquainted with the city than he, and he did not succeed in catching them. Finally he gave it up, and, sitting down on a convenient door-step, gave himself up to melancholy reflections.

CHAPTER XV.

ANY WAY TO MAKE A LIVING.

Boys who have a good home are apt to undervalue it. They do not realize the comfort of having their daily wants provided for without any anxiety on their part. They are apt to fancy that they would like to go out into the great world to seek their fortunes. Sometimes it may be necessary and expedient to leave the safe anchorage of home, and brave the dangers of the unknown sea; but no boy should do this without his parents' consent, nor then, without making up his mind that he will need all his courage and all his resolution to obtain success.

Sam found himself penniless in a great city, and with no way open, that he could think of, to earn money. Even the business of the boot-black, humble as it is, required a small capital to buy a brush and box of blacking. So, too, a newsboy must pay for his papers when he gets them, unless he is well known. So Sam, sitting on the door-step, felt that he was in a tight place. Where was he to get his dinner from? He did not care to repeat his operation of the morning, for it was not pleasant to be "bounced."

"I wonder if I couldn't get a chance in a store," he thought. "That wouldn't need any money. There seems to be a lot of stores in the city. I guess there must be a place for me somewhere."

This thought encouraged Sam. He rose from his lowly seat, and determined to look about for a place. Presently he came to a real-estate office. Sam did not understand very well what kind of a business that was, but on the window a piece of paper was pasted, on which was written, "A Boy Wanted."

"I guess I'll go in," thought Sam. "Maybe they'll take me."

There were three boys ahead of him; but they were not very eligible-looking specimens. So they were dismissed with small ceremony, and Sam was beckoned to the desk.

"I suppose you have come about the place," said

a man with black whiskers, and a pen behind his ear.

"Yes," answered Sam.

"How old are you?"

"Twelve."

"Rather young. Still you are large of your age."

"I am pretty strong," said Sam, anxious to succeed in his application.

"There isn't any work to be done that requires strength," said the black-whiskered man. "How is your education?"

"Pretty good," said Sam, with hesitation.

"Do you live in the city?"

"Yes, sir."

"With your parents?"

"No, sir. They are dead."

"That is an objection. Perhaps, however, you live with an aunt or uncle. That will answer as well."

"Yes," said Sam, determined to obviate this objection. "I live with my uncle."

"Where does he live?"

"In New York," answered Sam.

"Don't you understand me? I mean to ask the street and number."

Sam was posed. He could not at the moment think of the name of any street except Broadway. But it would not do to hesitate. So he said promptly, "He lives at No. 656 Broadway."

"What is his business?" inquired the black-whiskered man.

"He keeps a store," answered Sam, feeling that he was getting deeper and deeper into the mire.

"What sort of a store?"

"A grocery store."

"What, at 656 Broadway?" demanded the other, in surprise. "I didn't know there was a grocery store in that neighborhood."

"Oh, murder!" thought Sam. "I'm found out." He made no answer, because he could not think of any.

"Why don't your father give you a place in his own store?" asked the real-estate agent, with some suspicion in his tone.

"He's got all the help he wants," said Sam, quickly.

Here another boy entered the office, a boy neatly dressed, and intelligent in appearance.

"Sit down a moment," said the agent to Sam, "while I speak with this other lad."

Sam took a seat, and listened to the conversation with the other boy. The conclusion of the matter was, that the other boy was engaged and Sam was obliged to go out to offer his services in some other quarter.

"What a lot of lies I had to tell!" he reflected. "What's the use of their asking so many questions? I don't see. I'll have to try somewhere else."

As Sam was sauntering along he was accosted by a tall man, evidently from the country.

"Boy, can you direct me to the 'Tribune' office?"

"Yes, sir," said Sam, "but it's some ways from here. It'll be worth ten cents to lead you there."

The gentleman hesitated.

"Well," he said after a pause, "I'll give it to you."

"Will you give it to me now?" asked Sam.

"I will pay you when you have done your work."

"The reason I asked was, because I showed a man the other day, and then he wouldn't pay me."

"That was mean," said the stranger. "I hope you don't think I would serve you so."

"Oh, no, sir. You're a gentleman," said Sam. "You wouldn't cheat a poor boy that hasn't had any breakfast this mornin'."

"Dear me! you don't say so?" ejaculated the compassionate stranger, shocked at Sam's fiction. "Here, take this twenty-five cents. Do you often have to go without your breakfast?"

"Often, sir," said Sam, unblushingly. "It's hard times for poor boys like me."

"There's another quarter," said the stranger, his compassion still more deeply moved.

Sam did feel some compunction now, for he was about to make a very poor return for the kindness of his new acquaintance. The fact was, he had not the slightest idea where the "Tribune" office was, and he had therefore undertaken what he was unable to perform. But he had gone too far to recede. Besides, he did not feel prepared to give up the money which he had obtained through false pretences. So counterfeiting a confidence which he did not feel he led the way up Centre street, saying, "This way, sir. "I'll lead you right to the office."

"I never was at the office," said the stranger, "though I've been a subscriber to the weekly 'Tribune' for ten years."

"That's a good while," said Sam.

"It is indeed, my boy. I live in Illinois, more than a thousand miles from this city. Indeed, I have never been in New York before."

"Haven't you?"

"No; now you, I suppose, my young friend, know your way all about the city."

"Of course I do," said Sam, in an off-hand manner.

"If I had more time, I would get you to guide me round the city," said the stranger.

"Wouldn't I lead you a wild-goose chase, old gentleman?" thought Sam. "You'd be pretty well taken in, I guess."

"I am obliged to go away to-night," continued the old gentleman, "but I thought I would renew my subscription to the 'Tribune' before I went."

"All right, sir; it's a nice paper," said Sam, who had never read a line in the "Tribune."

"So I think. Are we almost at the office?"

"Almost," said Sam. "If you don't mind waiting I'll run over and speak to my cousin a minute."

There was a boot-black on the opposite side of the street. It struck Sam, who did not like to deceive so generous a patron, that he could obtain the information he needed of this boy.

"Can you tell me where the 'Tribune' office is?" he asked hurriedly.

The boot-black had no more scruples about lying than Sam, and answered, glibly, pointing to the Tombs prison, a little farther on, "Do you see that big stone buildin'?"

"Yes," said Sam.

"That's it."

"Thank you," said Sam, feeling relieved, and never doubting the correctness of this statement.

He returned to the stranger, and said, cheerfully, "We're almost there."

"Is that boy your cousin?" asked his acquaintance.

"Yes," said Sam.

"He blacks boots for a living."

"Yes, sir."

"Does he do well at it?"

"Pretty well."

"Did you ever black boots?"

"No, sir," answered Sam, telling the truth by way of variety.

"That's the 'Tribune' office," said Sam, a moment later, pointing to the gloomy-looking prison.

"Is it?" echoed the stranger, in surprise. "Really, it's a very massive structure."

"Yes," said Sam, mistaking the word employed, "it's very *massy*."

"It doesn't look much like a newspaper office."

For the first time Sam began to suspect that he had been deceived, and he naturally felt in a hurry to get away.

"You go right in," he said, confidently, "and they'll attend to you inside. Now I'll go and get some breakfast."

"To be sure. You must be hungry."

The stranger walked up the massive steps, and Sam hurried away.

"I wonder what place that is, anyhow," he said to himself. "Now I've got money enough for dinner."

For a country boy Sam was getting along fast.

CHAPTER XVI.

SAM MEETS BROWN AND IS UNHAPPY.

NEVER doubting Sam's assurance, the stranger entered the gloomy building, the lower part of which is divided into court-rooms. Out of one of these a man came, to whom he addressed this question: "Where is the counting-room?"

"The counting-room!" repeated the man, staring. "There isn't any here, that I know of."

"I want to subscribe for the weekly edition," explained the man from Illinois.

"It strikes me you're a weakly edition of a man yourself," thought the other. "He must be a lunatic," was the next thought. "I may as well humor him."

"Go in at that door," he said.

The stranger entered as directed, and at once recognized it as a court-room.

"It is very singular that there should be a court-room in the 'Tribune' office," he thought. He took a seat, and whispered to a man at his side: "Can you tell me where the 'Tribune' office is?"

"Printing-house Square," was the whispered reply.

"Where's that?"

"Not much over a quarter of a mile from here."

"The boy deceived me," thought the stranger indignantly, "and I gave him fifty cents for doing it. He must be a young rascal."

"What building is this?" he asked, still in a whisper.

"The Tombs."

"What, the prison!"

"Yes; didn't you know it?" asked the informant, in surprise.

"I am a stranger in the city," said the Illinois man apologetically.

"Did you want to go to the 'Tribune' office?"

"Yes; I wished to subscribe for the paper."

"I am going that way. I will show you if you desire it."

"Thank you. I shall consider it a favor."

So the two retraced their steps, and this time our

Illinois friend found the office of which he was in quest. He came near finding Sam also, for as he stood in front of French's Hotel, he saw his recent acquaintance approaching, and quickly dodged inside the hotel till he had passed. A boot-black to whom he had been speaking followed him in surprise.

"I say, what's up, Johnny?" he asked. "Yer didn't see a copp, did yer?"

"No, it's that man that just went by."

"Who's he?"

"He's the man I ran away from," said Sam, not caring to tell the truth.

"What would he do if he should catch you?" asked the boot-black, with curiosity.

"Lick me," said Sam, laconically.

"Then you did right. Is he going to stay here long?"

"No; he's going away to-day."

"Then you're safe. You'd better go the other way from him."

"So I will," said Sam. "Where's the Park I've heard so much about?"

"Up that way."

"Is it far?"

"Four or five miles."

"It's a long way to walk."

"You can ride for five cents."

"Can I?"

"Yes; just go over to the Astor House, and take the Sixth avenue cars, and they'll take you there."

Sam had intended to spend his entire fifty cents in buying dinner when the time came, but he thought he would like to see Central Park. Besides, he would be safe from pursuit, and the punishment which he felt he deserved. Following the directions of his boy friend, he entered a Sixth avenue car, and in a little less than an hour was set down at one of the gates of the Park. He entered with a number of others, and followed the path that seemed most convenient, coming out at last at the lake. Until now Sam had thought rather slightingly of the Park. Green fields were no novelty to him, but he admired the lake with the boats that plied over its surface filled with lively passengers. He would have invested ten cents in a passage ticket; but he felt that if he did this, he must sacrifice a part of his intended dinner, and Sam was growing prudent. He wandered about the Park two or three hours, sitting down at times on the benches that are to be found here and there for the convenience of visitors. He felt ready to go back; but it was only noon, and he was not sure but he might fall in with the gentleman from Illinois, whom he had left at the entrance of the Tombs.

He was destined to meet an acquaintance, but this time it was some one that had cheated him. Looking up from the bench on which he was seated, he saw his host of the preceding night, Mr. Clarence Brown, lounging along, smoking a cigar, with a look of placid contentment on his face.

"That cigar was bought with my money," thought Sam, bitterly; and in this conclusion he was right.

Sam jumped from his seat, and advanced to meet his enemy.

"Look here, Mr. Brown!"

Clarence Brown started as he saw who addressed him, for he was far from expecting to meet Sam here. He saw from the boy's looks that he was suspected of robbing him, and decided upon his course.

"Oh, it's you, is it?" he said, smiling. "How do you like the Park?"

"Never mind about that," said Sam, impatiently. "I want my money."

Mr. Brown arched his eyes in surprise.

"Really, my young friend, I don't comprehend you," he said, withdrawing his cigar from his mouth. "You speak as if I owed you some money."

"Quit fooling!" said Sam, provoked at the other's coolness. "I want that money you took from me while I was asleep last night."

"It strikes me you have been dreaming," said Brown, composedly. "I don't know anything about your money. How much did you have?"

"Nearly seven dollars."

"Are you sure you had it when you went to bed?"

"Yes. I kept it in my vest-pocket."

"That was careless. You should have concealed it somewhere. I would have kept it for you if you had asked me."

"I dare say you would," said Sam, with withering sarcasm.

"Certainly, I wouldn't refuse so small a favor."

"Are you sure you didn't keep it for me?" said Sam.

"How could I, when you didn't give it to me?" returned the other, innocently.

"If you didn't take it," said Sam, rather staggered by the other's manner, "where did it go to?"

"I don't know, of course; but I shouldn't be surprised if it fell out of your vest-pocket among the bed-clothes. Did you look?"

"Yes."

"You might have overlooked it."

"Perhaps so," said Sam, thoughtfully.

He began to think he had suspected Mr. Brown unjustly. Otherwise, how could he be so cool about it?

"I am really sorry for your loss," said Brown, in a tone of sympathy; "all the more so, because I am hard up myself. I wish I had seven dollars to lend you."

"I wish you had," muttered Sam. "I can't get along without money."

"Did you have any breakfast?"

"Yes."

Sam did not furnish particulars, not liking to acknowledge the treatment he had received.

"Oh, you'll get along," said Brown, cheerfully. "Come and lodge with me again to-night."

"I don't know but what I will," said Sam, reflecting that he had no money to lose now, as he intended to spend all he had for dinner.

"Sit down and let us have a friendly chat," said Clarence Brown. "Won't you have a cigar? I've got an extra one."

"I never smoked," said Sam.

"Then it's time you learned. Shall I show you how?"

"Yes," said Sam.

The fact is, our very badly behaved hero had long cherished a desire to see how it seemed to smoke a cigar; but in the country he had never had the opportunity. In the city he was master of his own actions, and it occurred to him that he would never have a better opportunity. Hence his affirmative answer.

Clarence Brown smiled slightly to himself, for he anticipated fun. He produced the cigar, lighted it by his own, and gave Sam directions how to smoke. Sam proved an apt pupil, and was soon puffing away with conscious pride. He felt himself several years older. But all at once he turned pale, and drew the cigar from his mouth.

"What's the matter?" asked Brown, demurely.

"I — don't — know," gasped Sam, his eyes rolling; "I — feel — sick."

"Do you? Don't mind it; it'll pass off."

"I think I'm going to die," said Sam, in a hollow voice. "Does smoking ever kill people?"

"Not often," said Brown, soothingly.

"I think it's goin' to kill me," said Sam, mournfully.

"Lie down on the bench. You'll feel better soon."

Sam lay down on his back, and again he wished himself safely back at the deacon's. New York seemed to him a very dreadful place. His head ached; his stomach was out of tune, and he felt very unhappy.

"Lie here a little while, and you'll feel better," said his companion. "I'll be back soon."

He walked away to indulge in a laugh at his victim's expense, and Sam was left alone.

CHAPTER XVII.

TIM BRADY.

An hour passed, and Clarence Brown did not reappear. He had intended to do so, but reflecting that there was no more to be got out of Sam changed his mind.

Sam lay down on the bench for some time, then raised himself to a sitting posture. He did not feel so sick as at first, but his head ached unpleasantly.

"I won't smoke any more," he said to himself. "I didn't think it would make me feel so bad."

I am sorry to say that Sam did not keep the resolution he then made; but at the time when he is first introduced to the reader, in the first chapter, had become a confirmed smoker.

"Why don't Mr. Brown come back?" he thought, after the lapse of an hour.

He waited half an hour longer, when he was brought to the conviction that Brown had played him false, and was not coming back at all. With this conviction his original suspicion revived, and he made up his mind that Brown had robbed him after all.

"I'd like to punch his head," thought Sam, angrily.

It did not occur to him that the deacon, from whom the money was originally taken, had the same right to punch his head. As I have said, Sam's conscience was not sensitive, and self-interest blinded him to the character of his own conduct.

His experience in smoking had given him a distaste for the Park, for this afternoon at least, and he made his way to the horse-cars determined to return. It did make him feel a little forlorn to reflect that he had no place to return to; no home but the streets. He had not yet contracted that vagabond feeling which makes even them seem homelike to the hundreds of homeless children who wander about in them by day and by night.

He was in due time landed at the Astor House. It was about four o'clock in the afternoon, and he had had nothing to eat since breakfast. But for the cigar, he would have had a hearty appetite. As it was, he felt faint, and thought he should relish some tea and toast. He made his way, therefore, to a restaurant in Fulton street, between Broadway and Nassau streets. It was a very respectable place, but at that time in the afternoon there were few at the tables. Sam had forty cents left. He found that this would allow him to buy a cup of tea, a plate of beefsteak, a plate of toast, and a piece of pie. He disposed of them, and going up to the desk paid his bill. Again he found himself penniless.

"I wonder where I am going to sleep," he thought. "I guess I'll ask some boot-blacks where they live. They can't afford to pay much."

The tea made his head feel better; and, though he was penniless, he began to feel more cheerful than an hour before.

He wandered about till he got tired, leaning against a building sometimes. He began to feel lonely. He knew nobody in the great city except Clarence Brown, whom he did not care to meet again, and the boot-black whose acquaintance he had made the day before.

"I wish I had some other boy with me," thought Sam; "somebody I knew. It's awful lonesome."

Sam was social by temperament, and looked about him to see if he could not make some one's acquaintance. Sitting on the same bench with him — for he was in City Hall Park — was a boy of about his own age apparently. To him Sam determined to make friendly overtures.

"What is your name, boy?" asked Sam.

The other boy looked round at him. He was very much freckled, and had a sharp look which made him appear preternaturally old.

"What do you want to know for?" he asked.

"I don't know anybody here. I'd like to get acquainted."

The street boy regarded him attentively to see if he were in earnest, and answered, after a pause, "My name is Tim Brady. What's yours?"

"Sam Barker."

"Where do you live?"

"Nowhere," said Sam. "I haven't got any home, nor any money."

"That's nothing!" said Tim. "No more have I."

"Haven't you?" said Sam, surprised. "Then where are you going to sleep to-night?"

"I know an old wagon, up an alley, where I can sleep like a top."

"Aint you afraid of taking cold, sleeping out of doors?" asked Sam, who, poor as he had always been, had never been without a roof to cover him.

"Take cold!" repeated the boy, scornfully. "I aint a baby. I don't take cold in the summer."

"I shouldn't think you could sleep in a wagon."

"Oh, I can sleep anywhere," said Tim. "It makes no difference to me where I curl up."

"Is there room enough in the wagon for me?" asked Sam.

"Yes, unless some other chap gets ahead of us."

"May I go with you?"

"In course you can."

"Suppose we find somebody else ahead of us."

"Then we'll go somewhere else. There's plenty of places. I say, Johnny, haven't you got no stamps at all?"

"Stamps!"

"Yes, money. Don't you know what stamps is?"

"No. I spent my last cent for supper."

"If you'd got thirty cents we'd go to the theatre."

"What theatre?"

"The Old Bowery."

"Is it good?"

"You bet!"

"Then I wish I had money enough to go. I neve. went to the theatre in my life."

"You didn't! Where was you raised?" said Tim, contemptuously.

"In the country."

"I thought so."

"They don't have theatres in the country."

"Then I wouldn't live there. It must be awful dull there."

"So it is," said Sam. "That's why I ran away."

"Did you run away?" asked Tim, interested. "Was it from the old man?"

"It was from the man I worked for. He wanted me to work all the time, and I got tired of it."

"What sort of work was it?" asked Tim.

"It was on a farm. I had to hoe potatoes, split wood, and such things."

"I wouldn't like it. It's a good deal more jolly bein' in the city."

"If you've only got money enough to get along," added Sam.

"Oh, you can earn money."

"How?" asked Sam, eagerly.

"Different ways."

"How do you make a livin'?"

"Sometimes I black boots, sometimes I sell papers, then again, I smash baggage."

"What's that?" asked Sam, bewildered.

"Oh, I forgot," exclaimed Tim. "You're from the country. I loaf round the depots and steamboat landin's, and carry carpet-bags and such things for pay."

"Is that smashing baggage?"

"*To* be sure."

"I could do that," said Sam, thoughtfully. "Can you make much that way?"

"'Pends on how many jobs you get, and whether the cove's liberal. Wimmen's the wust. They'll beat a chap down to nothin', if they can."

"How much do you get anyway for carrying a bundle?"

"I axes fifty cents, and generally gets a quarter. The wimmen don't want to pay more'n ten cents."

"I guess I'll try it to-morrow, if you'll tell me where to go."

"You can go along of me. I'm goin' smashin' myself to-morrer."

"Thank you," said Sam. "I'm glad I met you. You see I don't know much about the city."

"Didn't you bring no money with you?"

"Yes, but it was stolen."

"Was your pockets picked?"

"I'll tell you about it. I was robbed in my sleep."

So Sam told the story of his adventures with Clarence Brown. Tim listened attentively.

"He was smart, he was," said Tim, approvingly.

"He's a rascal," said Sam, hotly, who did not relish hearing his spoiler praised.

"Course he is, but he's smart too. You might a knowed he'd do it."

"How should I know? I thought he was a kind man, that wanted to do me a favor."

Tim burst out laughing.

"Aint you green, though?" he remarked. "Oh my eye, but you're jolly green."

"Am I?" said Sam, rather offended. "Is everybody a thief in New York?"

"Most everybody, if they gets a chance," said Tim, coolly. "Didn't you ever steal yourself?"

Sam colored. He had temporarily forgotten the little adventure that preceded his departure from his country home. After all, why should he be so angry with Clarence Brown for doing the very same thing he had done himself? Why, indeed? But Sam had an answer ready. The deacon did not need the money, while he could not get along very well without it. So it was meaner in Clarence Brown to take all he had, than in him to take what the deacon could so well spare.

I hope my readers understand that this was very flimsy and unsatisfactory reasoning. Stealing is stealing, under whatever circumstances. At any rate

Sam found it inconvenient to answer Tim's pointed question.

They talked awhile longer, and then his companion rose from the bench.

"Come along, Johnny," he said. "Let's go to roost."

"All right," said Sam, and the two left the Park.

CHAPTER XVIII.

SAM TURNS IMPOSTOR.

Tim conducted our hero to an alley-way, not far from the North river, in which an old wagon had come to temporary anchor.

"This is my hotel," he said. "I like it 'cause it's cheap. They don't trouble you with no bills here. Tumble in."

Tim, without further ceremony, laid himself down on the floor of the wagon, and Sam followed his example. There is everything in getting used to things, and that is where Tim had the advantage. He did not mind the hardness of his couch, while Sam, who had always been accustomed to a regular bed, did. He moved from one side to another, and then lay on his back, seeking sleep in vain.

"What's up?" muttered Tim, sleepily. "Why don't you shut your peepers?"

"The boards are awful hard," Sam complained.

"It aint nothin' when you're used to it," said Tim. "You go to sleep, and you won't mind it."

"I wish I could," said Sam, turning again.

Finally he succeeded in getting to sleep, but not till some time after his companion. He slept pretty well, however, and did not awaken till, at six o'clock, he was shaken by his companion.

"What's the matter? Where am I?" asked Sam, feeling bewildered at first.

"Why, here you are, in course," said the matter-of-fact Tim. "Did you think you was in the station-house?"

"No, I hope not," answered Sam. "What time is it?"

"I don't know. A chap stole my watch in the night. I guess it's after six. Have you got any stamps?"

"No."

"Nor I. We've got to stir round, and earn some breakfast."

"How'll we do it?"

"We'll go down to the pier, and wait for the Boston boat. Maybe we'll get a chance to smash some baggage."

"I hope so," said Sam, "for I'm hungry."

"I'm troubled that way myself," said Tim. "Come along."

When they reached the pier, they found a number of boys, men, and hack-drivers already in waiting. They had to wait about half an hour, when they saw the great steamer slowly approaching the wharf.

Instantly Tim was on the alert.

"When they begin to come ashore, you must go in and try your luck. Just do as I do."

This Sam resolved to do.

A tall man emerged from the steamer, bearing a heavy carpet-bag.

"Smash yer baggage?" said Tim.

"No, I think not. I can carry it myself."

"I haven't had any breakfast," said Tim, screwing up his freckled features into an expression of patient suffering.

"Nor I either," said the stranger, smiling.

"You've got money to buy some, and I haven't," said Tim, keeping at his side.

"Well, you may carry it," said the gentleman, good-naturedly.

Tim turned half round, and winked at Sam, as much as to say, "Did you see how I did it?"

Sam was quick enough to take the hint.

"Smash your carpet-bag?" he asked of a middle-aged lady, imitating as closely as possible Tim's professional accent.

"What?" asked the lady, startled.

"She don't understand," thought Sam. "Let me carry it for you, ma'am."

"I do not need it. I am going to take a cab."

"Let me take it to the cab," persisted Sam; but he was forestalled by a hack-driver who had heard the lady's remark.

"Let me take it, ma'am," he said, thrusting Sam aside. "I've got a nice carriage just outside. Take you anywhere you want to go."

So the lady was carried away, and Sam had to make a second application. This time he addressed himself to a gentleman whose little daughter walked by his side.

"No," said the gentleman; "the carpet-bag is small. I don't need help."

The smallness of the bag, by the way, was one reason why Sam, who did not like heavy bundles, wanted to carry it. He felt that it was time to practise on the stranger's feelings.

"I want to earn some money to buy bread for my mother," he whined, in a very creditable manner, considering how inexperienced he was.

This attracted the attention of the little girl, who, like most little girls, had a tender and compassionate heart.

"Is your mother poor?" she asked.

"Very poor," said Sam. "She hasn't got a cent to buy bread for the children."

"Have you got many brothers and sisters?" asked the little girl, her voice full of sympathy.

"Five," answered Sam, piteously.

"O papa," said the little girl, "let him take your carpet-bag. Think of it, his mother hasn't got anything to eat."

"Well, Clara," said her father, indulgently, "I

suppose I must gratify you. Here, boy, take the bag, and carry it carefully."

"All right, sir," said Sam, cheerfully.

"I guess I can get along," he thought, complacently. "That's a good dodge."

"When we get to Broadway, we'll take the stage," said the gentleman. "Take hold of my hand, tight, Clara, while we cross the street."

Clara seemed disposed to be sociable, and entered into conversation with the young baggage-smasher.

"Are your brothers and sisters younger than you?" she inquired.

"Yes," said Sam.

"How many of them are boys?"

"There's two boys besides me, and three girls," said Sam, readily.

"What are their names?" asked Clara.

"Why," answered Sam, hesitating a little, "there's Tom and Jim and John, and Sarah and Maggie."

"I don't see how that can be," said Clara, puzzled. "Just now you said there were three girls and only two boys."

"Did I?" said Sam, rather abashed. "I didn't think what I was saying."

"Isn't your father alive?" asked the little girl.

"No; he's dead."

"And do you have to support the family?"

"Yes; except what mother does."

"What does she do?"

"Oh, she goes out washing."

"Poor boy, I suppose you have a hard time."

"Yes," said Sam; "some days we don't get anything to eat."

"O papa, isn't it dreadful?" said Clara, her warm little heart throbbing with sympathy.

Her father was less credulous, and he was struck by Sam's hearty appearance. Certainly he looked very unlike a boy who did not have enough to eat.

"You don't look as if you suffered much from hunger, my boy," said he, with a penetrating look.

"I had a good dinner yesterday," said Sam. "A gentleman gave me some money for showing him the way to the 'Tribune' office."

"One dinner seems to have done you a great deal of good," said the man.

"It always does me good," said Sam, and here he had no occasion to tell a falsehood.

"I hope you carried some of the money home to your mother, and brothers and sisters."

"Yes, I did; I bought some meat, and mother cooked it. We don't often have meat."

"Perhaps I am doing the boy injustice," thought Mr. Glenham, for this was his name.

As for Clara, her childish sympathies were fully aroused.

"Papa," she said, "may I give this poor boy the half dollar Aunt Lucy gave me?"

"I thought you had arranged some way of spending it, Clara."

"So I had, papa; but I'd rather give it to this poor boy."

"You may do as you like, my darling," said her father, tenderly.

"Here, poor boy, take this home to your mother," said Clara.

My readers have probably inferred already that Sam was not a boy of very high principles, but I must do him the justice to say that he felt ashamed to take the money tendered him by the little girl upon whom he had imposed by his false story.

"I don't like to take your money," he said, hanging back.

"But I want you to," said Clara, eagerly. "I'd a great deal rather your mother would have it."

"You may take it," said Mr. Glenham, who was disposed to regard Sam with greater favor, on account of the reluctance he exhibited to profit by Clara's compassion.

"Thank you," said Sam, no longer withholding his hand. "You are very kind."

By this time they had reached Broadway, and Sam delivered up the bag.

Mr. Glenham handed him a quarter.

"That is for your trouble," he said.

"Thank you, sir," said Sam.

A Broadway stage came up, and they both were lost to view.

Sam was in good spirits over his good fortune.

"Seventy-five cents!" he said to himself.

"That's what I call luck. I don't believe Tim's done so well. It aint so hard to make your living in New York, after all. I guess I'll go and get some breakfast."

CHAPTER XIX.

HOW SAM FARED.

On the strength of his good luck, Sam provided himself with a good breakfast, which cost him forty cents. He felt pretty sure of earning something more during the day to add to the remaining thirty-five. But Fortune is capricious, and our hero found all his offers of service firmly refused. He tried again to excite compassion by his fictitious story of a starving family at home; but his appeals were made to the flinty-hearted or the incredulous. So, about two o'clock, he went to dinner, and spent the remainder of his money.

Again he spent the night with Tim in the wagon, and again in the morning he set out to earn his breakfast. But luck was against him. People insisted on carrying their own carpet-bags, to the great detriment of the baggage-smashing business. Tim was no luckier than Sam. About ten o'clock they were walking despondently through a side street, discussing ways and means.

"I'm awful hungry, Tim," said Sam, mournfully.

"So am I, you bet!"

"I wouldn't mind if I had a couple of apples," said Sam, fixing his eyes upon an old woman's apple-stand. "Wouldn't she trust?"

"Not much," said Tim. "You try her, if you want to."

"I will," said Sam, desperately.

The two boys approached the apple-stand.

"I say," said Sam to the wrinkled old woman who presided over it, "how do you sell your apples?"

"A penny a piece," she answered, in a cracked voice. "Is that cheap enough for ye?"

"I'll take five —," said Sam.

The old woman began eagerly to pick out the required number, but stopped short when he finished the sentence, — "if you'll trust me till afternoon."

"Is it trust ye?" she ejaculated suspiciously. "No farther than I can see yer. I'm up to your tricks, you young spalpeen, thryin' to chate a poor widder out of her money."

"I'll pay you sure," said Sam, "but I haven't earned anything yet to-day."

"Then it's I that can't be supportin' a big, strong boy like you. Go away and come back, whin you've got money."

Here Tim broke in.

"My friend always pays his bills," he said. "You needn't be afraid to trust him."

"And who are you?" asked the old woman. "I don't know you, and I can't take your word. You're tryin' the two of you to swindle a poor widder."

"My father's an alderman," said Tim, giving the wink to Sam.

"Is he now? Thin, let him lind your friend money, and don't ask a poor woman to trust."

"Well, I would, but he's gone to Washington on business."

"Thin, go after him, and lave me alone. I don't want no spalpeens like you round my apple-stand."

"Look here, old woman, I'll have you arrested for callin' me names. Come away, Sam; her apples are rotten anyhow."

The old woman began to berate them soundly,

indignant at this attack upon her wares; and in the midst of it the two boys walked off.

"We didn't make much," said Sam. "I'm awful hungry."

"Take that, then," said Tim, pulling an apple out of his pocket.

Sam opened his eyes.

"How did you get it?" he asked in astonishment.

Tim put his tongue in his cheek.

"I took it when you were talkin' to the ould woman," he answered; "and here's another."

So saying he produced a companion apple, and made a vigorous onslaught upon it, Sam following suit.

"I don't see how you could do it," said Sam, admiringly, "and she looking on all the time."

"It's easy enough when you know how," said Tim, complacently.

"She'd catch me, sure."

"Likely she would; you aint used to it."

Sam ought to have felt uneasy at appropriating the result of a theft; but his conscience was an easy one, and he felt hungry. So he made short work of the apple, and wished for more.

"I wish you'd taken two apiece," he said.

"I couldn't," said Tim. "She'd have seen 'em stickin' out of my pocket, and called a copp."

"One's better than none; I feel a little better," said Sam, philosophically. "I 'spose it's stealing, though."

"Oh, what's the odds? She'll never miss 'em. Come along."

In the course of the forenoon Sam managed to earn ten cents, and was forced to content himself with a very economical dinner. There was a place on Ann street, where, for this small sum, a plate of meat and a potato were furnished, but enough only to whet the appetite of a hearty boy like Sam. A suspicion did enter his mind as he rose from the table penniless once more, and his appetite still unsatisfied, that he had bought his liberty dearly, if his affairs did not improve. In the country he had enough to eat, a good bed to sleep in, and no care or anxiety, while he was not overworked. Here there was constant anxiety, and he never knew, when he rose in the morning, where his dinner was to come from, or whether he would be able to buy one. Still there was a fascination in the free, lawless life, and if he could only be sure of making even fifty cents a day he would probably have preferred it.

It is not necessary to describe Sam's life in detail for the next month. He and Tim were constant companions; and under Tim's instruction he was rapidly acquiring the peculiar education of a street vagabond. Of his employments in that brief period it would be difficult to give a complete list. At one time he blacked boots for another boy, to whom he paid half his receipts, in return for the use of the box and blacking. But Sam was detected by his employer in rendering a false account, and was thrown upon his own resources again. It would have been much more to his interest to have a blacking-brush and box of his own; but whenever Sam had capital enough he preferred to spend it for a good dinner, so there did not seem much chance of his getting ahead. He had, before this time, been introduced to the Newsboys' Lodging House, where he was interrogated about his past life by the superintendent.

Sam was obliged to have recourse to his imagination in reply, feeling that if he spoke the truth he would be liable to be returned to his country home.

"Are your parents living?" inquired Mr. O'Connor.

"No," said Sam, telling the truth this time.

"When did they die?"

"Two years ago."

"Did they die in New York?"

"Yes, sir. They died of small-pox," volunteered Sam.

"And have you been supporting yourself since then?"

"Yes, sir."

"How does it happen that you have not been round here before?"

"I was living with my uncle," answered Sam, hesitating.

"Why have you left him?"

"He didn't treat me well."

"Perhaps you didn't behave well."

"Oh, yes, I did."

"What is your uncle's name?"

"James Cooper."

"Where does he live, — in what street?"

"He's moved away from the city now," said Sam, feeling that he must put a stop to these inconvenient inquiries.

So Sam was admitted to the privileges of the lodging-house. Now, he found it much easier to get along. For eighteen cents a day he was provided with lodging, breakfast and supper, and it was not often that he could not obtain as much as that. When he could earn enough more to buy a "square meal" in the middle of the day, and a fifteen-cent ticket to the pit of the Old Bowery theatre in the evening, he felt happy. He was fairly adrift in the streets of the great city, and his future prospects did not look very brilliant. It is hardly necessary to say that in a moral point of view he had deteriorated rather than improved. In fact, he was fast developing into a social outlaw, with no particular scruples against lying or stealing. One thing may be said in his favor, he never made use of his strength to oppress a younger boy. On the whole, he was good-natured, and not at all brutal. He had on one occasion interfered successfully to protect a young boy from one of greater strength who was beating him. I like to mention this, because I do not like to have it supposed that Sam was wholly bad.

We will now advance the story some months, and see what they have done for Sam.

To begin with, they have not improved his wardrobe. When he first came to the city he was neatly though coarsely dressed; now his clothes hang in rags about him, and, moreover, they are begrimed with mud and grease. His straw hat and he have some time since parted company, and he now wears a greasy article which he picked up at a second-hand store in Baxter street for twenty-five cents. If Sam were troubled with vanity, he might feel disturbed by his disreputable condition; but as he sees plenty of other boys of his own class no better dressed, he thinks very little about it. Such as they are, his clothes are getting too small for him, for Sam has grown a couple of inches since he came to the city.

Such was our hero's appearance when one day he leaned against a building on Broadway, and looked lazily at the vehicles passing, wishing vaguely that he had enough money to buy a square meal. A Broadway stage was passing at the time. A small man, whose wrinkled face indicated that he was over sixty, attempted to descend from the stage while in motion. In some way he lost his footing, and, falling, managed to sprain his ankle, his hat falling off and rolling along on the pavement.

Sam, who was always on the lookout for chances, here saw an opening. He dashed forward, lifted the old gentleman to his feet, and ran after his hat, and restored it.

"Are you hurt?" he asked.

"I think I have sprained my ankle. Help me up-stairs to my office," said the old man.

He pointed to a staircase leading up from the side-walk.

"All right," said Sam. "Lean on me."

CHAPTER XX.

SAM GETS INTO A NEW BUSINESS.

Sam helped the old man up two flights of stairs.

"Shall we go any farther?" he asked.

"No; that's my office," said his companion, pointing to a door, over which was the number 10. From his pocket he drew a key, and opened the door. Sam entered with him. The room was small. One corner was partitioned off for an inner office. Inside was a chair, something like a barber's chair, and a table covered with instruments. Sam's curiosity was aroused. He wondered what sort of business was carried on here. He also wondered whether he would get anything for his trouble.

"If you don't want me any longer I'll go," he said, by way of a delicate hint.

"Stop a minute," said the old man, who had limped to a sofa in the outer office, and sat down.

"I guess I'll get something," thought Sam, cheerfully complying with the request.

"What do you do for a living?" asked the old man.

"Sometimes I black boots, sometimes I sell papers, — anything that'll pay."

"What are you doing now?"

"Nothing. Business aint good."

"Would you like something to do?"

Sam gave a glance into the office, and answered dubiously, "Yes." He was not at all clear about the nature of the employment likely to be offered.

"Then I may be able to give you a job. Do you know my business?"

"No, sir."

"I'm a corn-doctor — you've heard of Dr. Felix Graham, the celebrated corn-doctor, haven't you?" said the old man, complacently.

"Yes," said Sam, thinking that this was the answer expected.

"I am Dr. Graham," said the old man, proudly.

"Are you?" said Sam in some curiosity.

"Yes. Now I'll tell you what I want you to do. Go and bring me that pile of circulars."

He pointed to a pile of papers on the floor in the corner.

Sam brought them as directed.

"Can you read?" asked the doctor.

"Yes, sir, a little."

"Read that circular."

Sam read as follows: —

"DR. FELIX GRAHAM,

CHIROPODIST.

Corns and bunions cured without pain.

Satisfaction guaranteed.

BROADWAY, ROOM 10."

Sam bungled over the word chiropodist, but was put right by the doctor.

"I want a boy to stand at the door, and distribute these circulars," said Dr. Graham. "Can you do it?"

"Of course I can," said Sam. "What pay will I get?"

"Ten cents a hundred;" said the doctor, "but you mustn't do as my last boy did."

"How did he do?" asked Sam.

"He was so anxious to get rid of them that he gave half a dozen away at a time. I caught him in it. He wanted to earn money too fast."

"He was smart," said Sam, with a grin.

"I don't like that kind of smartness," said the doctor, sharply. "I want you to serve me faithfully."

"So I will," said Sam.

"You needn't give to everybody. There isn't much use in giving to children."

"Yes, sir."

"But if you see any one walking as if he had corns, be sure to hand him one."

"Yes, sir."

"Now count off a hundred of the circulars, and go downstairs."

"All right, sir."

This was the first regular employment Sam had obtained, and he felt rather important. He resolved to acquit himself to the satisfaction of the doctor. In his zeal he even determined to improve upon his instructions.

He had no sooner taken his stand than he saw a

gentleman and lady approaching. They were young, and, being engaged, were indulging in conversation more interesting to themselves than any one else. The gentleman had on a pair of tight boots, and from his style of walking Sam concluded that he was a suitable customer.

"Here, sir," said he, pressing a circular into the young man's gloved hand.

"What's that?" asked the young man. Then, glancing at it, he showed it with a laugh to the young lady.

"Look here, boy," he said turning to Sam, "what made you give me this?"

"You walked as if you'd got corns," said Sam, honestly. "Walk right up, and Dr. Graham will cure 'em in a jiffy."

"Perhaps you'll tell me what is to become of this young lady while I go up, Johnny?"

"Maybe she's got corns too," said Sam. "She can go up too."

Both the lady and gentleman laughed convulsively, considerably to Sam's surprise, for he was not aware that he had said anything unusual or funny.

"Shall we go up, Eliza?" asked the young man.

The only answer was a laugh, and they passed on.

The next one who attracted Sam's attention was an elderly maiden lady.

"Have you got corns, ma'am?" asked Sam, eagerly.

Now it so happened that the lady was a little deaf, and did not understand Sam's question. Unfortunately for herself, she stopped short, and inquired, "What did you say?"

"I guess she's hard of hearing," Sam concluded, and raising his voice loud enough to be heard across the street, he repeated his question: "HAVE YOU GOT CORNS, MA'AM?"

At the same time he thrust a circular into the hand of the astonished and mortified lady.

Two school-girls, just behind, heard the question, and laughed heartily. The offended lady dropped the paper as if it were contamination, and sailed by, her sallow face red with anger.

"That's funny," thought Sam. "I don't know what's got into all the people. Seems to me they're ashamed of havin' corns."

The next half-dozen took circulars, mechanically glanced at them, and dropped them indifferently.

"Guess they aint got corns," thought the observing Sam.

By and by a countryman came along, and into his hand Sam put the circular.

"What's this?" he asked.

"It's corns. Just go upstairs, and the doctor'll cure 'em less'n no time."

"Wal, I have got two," said the countryman. "They hurt like time too. What does this doctor charge?"

Sam did not know, but he was not the boy to allow his ignorance to appear.

"Ten cents apiece," he answered.

"That's cheap enough, anyway," said he. "I've got a good mind to go up. Where is it?"

"Come along. I'll show you," said Sam, promptly.

"I guess I may as well. Are you sure he can cure 'em?"

"I ought to know," said Sam. "I had one about

as big as a marble on my big toe. The doctor, he cured it in a minute."

"You don't say! He must be pooty good."

"You bet! He's the great Dr. Graham. Everybody's heard of him."

By such convincing assurances the man's faith was increased. He followed Sam into the doctor's office.

"Here," said Sam, "I've brought you a customer, Dr. Graham. I told him you could cure his corns in a jiffy."

The doctor smiled approvingly.

"You are right there. My friend, sit down in this chair."

"You won't hurt, will you, doctor?" asked the customer, glancing with a little alarm at the table with its instruments.

"Oh, no, you'll scarcely feel it."

Sam returned to his post, and began to distribute handbills once more.

About quarter of an hour later he was assailed by an angry voice. Looking up, he saw the customer he had sent upstairs.

"Look here, boy," he said, angrily; "you told me a lie."

"How did I?" asked Sam.

"You told me the doctor only charged ten cents for each corn. Jerusalem! he made me fork out a dollar."

Sam was rather surprised himself at the price.

"I guess they was tough ones, mister," he said. "He cured 'em, didn't he?"

"Ye—es."

"Then it's worth the money. You don't want 'em back, do you?"

"No," admitted the other; "but it's a thunderin' sight to pay;" and he went off grumbling.

"Don't the doctor make money, though?" thought Sam. "He'd orter give me a commission on them two dollars."

CHAPTER XXI.

SAM OBTAINS A PLACE.

HAVING disposed of his circulars, Sam went up to the office.

"Have you distributed all the circulars?" asked the doctor.

"Yes, sir."

"Well, here's the ten cents I promised you."

Sam took it, but stood his ground.

"I sent you up a customer," he said.

"A patient; yes."

"And you made two dollars out of him."

"Who told you?"

"He did."

"I charged him my regular price. What of that?" asked the doctor, not comprehending Sam's meaning.

"He wouldn't have come up if it hadn't been for me. I think I'd ought to have a commission."

"Oh, that's it," said the doctor. "That doesn't follow. He came up because of the circular."

"No, he didn't," said Sam. "He came up because I told him what a great doctor you was."

The doctor thought over Sam's proposal, and, being a sharp man, he decided that it was for his advantage to secure an alliance with him.

"You are right," he said. "You are entitled to something."

Sam brightened up.

"Here is a quarter in addition to the ten cents I just gave you."

"Thank you, sir," said Sam, gratified.

"Shall I go down, and give away some more circulars?" he asked.

"Yes; I'll give you another hundred. Don't give them away too fast. It's of no use to give to children."

"All right, sir."

So Sam went down into the street. The first passer-by was a boy of twelve.

"Give me one of them papers," he said.

Rather to his surprise Sam did not immediately comply. He first asked a question.

"Have you got a dollar?"

"A dollar! You don't want a dollar for that paper, do you?"

"No; but I aint goin' to waste it on you unless you've got a dollar."

"What do I want of a dollar?" asked the boy, surprised.

"To pay for havin' your corn cured."

The boy burst into a laugh.

"I aint got no corns," he said.

"Then go along, and don't bother me. You're no good."

A young dandy advanced, dressed in the height of fashion, swinging a light cane in his lavender-gloved hand. A rose was in his button-hole, and he was just in the act of saluting a young lady, when Sam thrust a circular into his hand.

"Go right upstairs," he said, "and get your corns cured. Only a dollar."

The young lady burst into a ringing laugh, and the mortified dandy reddened with mortification.

"Keep your dirty paper to yourself, boy," he said. "I am not troubled with those — ah, excrescences."

"I never heard of them things," said Sam. "I said corns."

"Stand out of my way, boy, or I'll cane you," exclaimed the incensed fop.

"Your cane wouldn't hurt," said Sam, regarding the slight stick with disdain. "Never mind; you needn't go up. I don't believe you've got a dollar."

This was rather impudent in Sam, I acknowledge; and the dandy would have been glad to chastise him.

"Miss Winslow," he said, "I hope you won't mind the rudeness of this — ah, ragamuffin."

"Oh, I don't," said the young lady, merrily; "he amuses me."

"So he does me; ha, ha! very good joke," said the dandy, laughing too, but not very merrily. "I hope you are quite well to-day."

"Thank you, quite so. But don't let me detain you, if you have an engagement upstairs."

"I assure you," protested the young man, hurriedly, "that I have no intention of going up at all."

"Then I must say good-morning, at any rate, as I am out shopping;" and the young lady passed on.

"I've a great mind to flog you," said the dandy, frowning at Sam. "I would if you wasn't so dirty. I wouldn't like to soil my hands by taking hold of you."

"That's lucky for you," said Sam, coolly.

The answer was a withering frown, but Sam was tough, and not easily withered.

"Aint he stuck up, though?" thought he, as the young man left him. "He don't seem to like me much."

"Have you got any corns, sir?" he asked, thrusting a paper into the hands of a portly gentleman with a merry face.

The gentleman laughed.

"Really, my boy," he said, "that is a very singular question."

"Is it?" said Sam. "I don't know why."

"Why do you ask?"

"Because Dr. Graham upstairs will cure you before you know it. It's only a dollar."

"You are sure you are not Dr. Graham, yourself?" said the stout man, regarding Sam with an amused expression.

"If I was, I'd wear better clothes," said Sam. "He makes lots of money, the doctor does."

"You'd better learn the business, my young friend."

"I guess I will, if he'll learn me," said Sam. "It'll pay better than standin' here, givin' away papers."

"Don't that pay?"

"Not very well," said Sam. "I only get ten cents a hundred."

"Can you pay your board out of that?"

"No, but I make commissions, besides," said Sam.

"How is that?" asked the stout gentleman, in some curiosity.

"If you'd gone upstairs, and had two corns cured, the doctor, — he'd have given me a quarter."

"Would he really?"

"Yes, he would. Hadn't you better go?"

"I have no occasion for Dr. Graham's services, at present," said the gentleman, laughing, "but still I don't want you to lose by me. Here's a quarter," producing the same from his vest-pocket, and giving it to Sam. "Isn't that just as well as if I had gone up?"

"Thank you, sir. You're a gentleman," said Sam. "Do you come by here often?"

His new acquaintance laughed. "Every day," he answered, "but I don't give away quarters every day. If you expect that, I am afraid I shall have to walk on the other side of the street. Good-morning, and success to you."

"Good-mornin'," said Sam.

"Well, here's luck," thought Sam. "I like this business pretty well. I've made sixty cents already, and the doctor's goin' to pay me ten cents more. That'll buy me a good, square dinner, and take me to the Old Bowery besides."

So Sam continued distributing his circulars. Some into whose hands they were thrust did not appear to be suitably grateful; and, though on the lookout for a customer, he did not succeed in finding any, till by good luck the last circular was placed in the hands of a man who was in search of just the relief which it promised.

"Where is Dr. Graham's office?" he inquired.

"Right upstairs, No. 10," said Sam, eagerly. "You just follow me, I'll show you."

"I think I can find it without you," said the other.

"Oh, I can go up just as well as not," said Sam, who had a special object, as we know, in serving as guide.

"Very well. Go ahead, and I will follow you."

Upstairs went Sam, the new patient following him.

"I've brought another," said Sam, as he burst into the office.

The doctor, though glad of another patient, was rather vexed at the style of Sam's announcement.

"Very well," he said. "Sit down there, till I have leisure to attend to you."

"All right, sir," said Sam, sitting down on the sofa in the outer office, and taking up the morning "Herald."

In twenty minutes the patient departed, relieved.

"Now," said Dr. Graham, addressing Sam, "I

have something to say to you. When you bring in a patient again, don't break out as you did just now: 'I've brought another.' I was very much mortified."

"What shall I say, then?" asked Sam.

"You needn't say anything, except 'This is Dr. Graham, sir.'"

"Very well," said Sam, "I'll remember. How much did you make out of him?"

"Don't speak in that way. My charges were three dollars."

"How much are you going to give me?"

"There's thirty cents."

"I think I'll go and get some dinner, now," said Sam. "Will you want me to-morrow?"

"I've been thinking," said the doctor, "that I would engage you as my office-boy."

"What would I have to do?"

"Stay in the office when I am away, and distribute circulars when I want you to."

"How much will you pay me?"

"Three dollars a week."

"And commissions too?"

"No; we'll say four days without commissions."

"All right, sir. I'll be on hand to-morrow mornin'."

"I've got a place, at last," thought Sam, in exultation. "Now, I'll go to dinner."

CHAPTER XXII.

THE YOUNG DOCTOR.

THE fact that he had obtained a place gave Sam a new sense of importance. Having drifted about the city streets for six months, never knowing in the morning where his meals were to come from during the day, or whether he was to have any, it was pleasant to think that he was to have regular wages. He presented himself in good season the next morning.

He was waiting outside when the doctor arrived.

"So you are on hand," said Dr. Graham.

"Yes, sir."

"By the way, what is your name?"

"Sam Barker."

"Very well, Sam, come upstairs with me."

Sam followed the doctor to his office.

The doctor surveyed his young assistant with critical eyes.

"Where do you buy your clothes?" he asked.

"I haven't bought any," said Sam. "I brought these from the country."

"They seem to be considerably the worse for wear. In fact, your appearance doesn't do credit to my establishment."

"I do look rather ragged," said Sam; "but I haven't got enough money to buy any new clothes."

"I have a son two years older than you. He may have some old clothes that would suit you. I'll have a bundle made up, and brought down to the office to-morrow."

"Thank you, sir," said Sam.

The doctor kept his promise, and the next day our hero was enabled to throw aside his rags, and attire himself in a neat gray suit, which considerably improved his outward appearance.

"Now," said the doctor, "I would suggest that a little more attention to washing would be of advantage to you."

"All right, sir; I'll remember."

Sam scrubbed himself to a considerable degree of

cleanness, and combed his hair. The ultimate result was a very creditable-looking office boy.

"Now," said the doctor, "I expect you to be faithful to my interests."

Sam readily promised this. Already he formed glowing anticipations of learning the business, and succeeding the doctor; or, at any rate, being admitted to partnership at some future day.

Several weeks passed by. Considering his previous course of life, Sam acquitted himself very well, He opened the office in the morning, swept it out, and got it in order before the doctor arrived. During the day he ran on errands, distributed circulars, in fact made himself generally useful. The doctor was rather irregular in coming in the morning, so that Sam was sometimes obliged to wait for him two or three hours. One morning, when sitting at his ease reading the morning paper, he was aroused by a knock at the door.

He rose and opened it.

"Is the doctor in?" asked a young man of Irish extraction.

"Hasn't come yet," said Sam. "Would you like to see him?"

"I would thin. He's the man that cures corns, isn't he?"

"Yes," said Sam. "He's the best corn-doctor in the city."

"Thin I've come to the right place, sure."

"Have you got one?"

"I've got a murtherin' big one. It almost kills me."

"Step in and wait for the doctor. He'll be in soon."

"I'm in a great hurry," said the young man. "It's porter I am in a store down town, and I can't stay long. How much does the doctor charge?"

"A dollar for each corn."

"O murder! does he now?"

"Isn't it worth that?"

"It's a mighty big price to pay."

"You see," said Sam, "he's a famous doctor; that's why he charges so much."

"I don't care for that at all. I'm a poor man, and it's hard on me payin' that much."

Here an idea struck Sam. He had often witnessed the doctor's operations, and to his inexperienced mind they seemed easy enough to perform. Why couldn't he operate a little on his own account before the doctor came? By so doing he would make a little money, and if successful he would have a future source of revenue, as patients often came when he was alone.

"I'm the doctor's assistant," he commenced.

"Are you now? So you're the young doctor?"

"Yes," said Sam.

"Then it's a mighty young doctor ye are."

"I know it," said Sam. "I've learnt the trade of Dr. Graham."

"Do you work at it mu h?" asked the patient.

"Yes," said Sam, "when the doctor's away. "I aint as good as he is," he admitted candidly, "and that is why I work cheaper."

"You work cheaper, do yer?"

"Yes," said Sam. "I only charge half price."

"That's fifty cents."

"Yes."

"And do you think you could cure me?"

"Of course I could," said Sam, confidently.

"Then go ahead," said the Irishman, in a fit of reckless confidence which he was destined to repent.

"Sit down there," said Sam, pointing out the patient's chair.

The patient obeyed.

"Now take off your boots. You don't think I can cut through the boot, do you?"

He was obeyed.

Sam began to fumble among the sharp instruments.

"What are you goin' to do?" asked the patient, rather alarmed.

"Oh, don't be afraid," said Sam. "You won't feel it."

"Won't feel the knife?"

"No, I'm goin to put on some liquid that'll take away the feeling."

"Shure you ought to know," said the patient, his confidence returning.

"Of course I do," said Sam.

"Now sit still."

Thus far Sam was perfectly self-possessed. He

went about his preparations witn an air that imposed upon the patient. But the difficulty was to come.

Things which look easy often are found difficult when attempted. When Sam began to wield the doctor's instruments he did so awkwardly. He lacked that delicacy of touch which can only be acquired by practice, and the result was tragical. The knife slipped, inflicting a deep gash, and causing a quick flow of blood.

"Oh, murder, I'm kilt!" exclaimed the terrified patient, bounding to his feet, and rushing frantically round the room. "I'm bladin' to death."

Sam was almost equally frightened. He stood, with the knife in his hand, panic-stricken.

"I'll have you up for murder, I will!" shouted Mr. Dennis O'Brien, clutching the wounded member. "Oh, why did I ever come to a boy doctor? Oh, whirra, whirra!"

"I didn't mean to do it," said Sam, frightened.

"You'll be hanged for killin' me, bad 'cess to you. Go for a doctor, quick."

Almost out of his wits Sam was about to obey, when as he opened the door he confronted his employer. Under ordinary circumstances he would have been sorry to have him come in so soon. Now he was glad.

"What's the meaning of all this?" asked Dr. Graham, surveying with astonishment the Irishman prancing around the office, and Sam's scared face.

"He's kilt me, doctor," said Dennis, groaning.

"He? Who?"

"The young doctor, shure."

"Who's he?"

"That's the one," said Mr. O'Brien, pointing to Sam. "He's cut my toe off, and I'm bladin' to death."

"What does this mean, Sam?" said the doctor, sternly.

"He was in a hurry," stammered Sam, "and I didn't want him to go away, so I thought I'd try to cure him, but the knife slipped, and —"

"I'll attend to your case afterwards. Sit down, sir."

"Will I die?" asked Dennis, lugubriously.

"No danger, now. You might, if I hadn't come just as I did."

Matters were soon remedied, and Dennis went away relieved, well satisfied because the doctor declined, under the circumstances, to receive any fee.

"Now, Sam," said the doctor, after he had gone, "what do you mean by such work as this?"

"I thought I could do it," said Sam, abashed.

"I ought to turn you away for this."

"It was only a mistake," said Sam.

"It came near being a very serious mistake. What would you have done if I had not come just as I did?"

"I don't know," said Sam.

"Never touch my instruments again. If you do I shall discharge you at once; that is, after giving you a sound flogging."

Sam felt that he had got off easily, and determined not to set up again as doctor on his own account

CHAPTER XXIII.

SAM FALLS INTO BAD COMPANY.

FOR a time matters went on smoothly. Sam was abashed by the result of his experiment, and discouraged from making another. He felt that he had a good place. Living chiefly at the lodging-house his expenses were small, and four dollars a week were ample to meet them. There was one thing he missed. however, — the freedom to roam about the streets at will. He felt this the more when the pleasant spring weather came on. There were times when he got sick of the confinement, and longed to leave the office.

It wâs a bright morning in May when Dr. Graham called from the inner office: —

"Sam."

"What, sir?"

"Do you know the way to Brooklyn?"

"Yes, sir."

"I want you to go over there for me."

"All right, sir."

It may be explained that Dr. Graham, on the first of May, had moved over to Brooklyn, and was occupying a house about a mile from Fulton Ferry.

"I want you to go to my house," said the doctor, "No. — H—— street, and carry this letter to my wife."

"Yes, sir."

"I forgot entirely to leave her some money to meet a bill; but if you go at once it will reach her in time. Stay, I will give you the address on a card."

"All right, sir."

"Here is a quarter. It will pay your car-fare, and over the ferry both ways. Now, mind you come back as quick as you can."

This Sam readily promised. He was glad to get away for the morning, as he calculated that the expedition would take him nearly, or quite, three hours. He took a car and got out at the Astor House. On his way down to the ferry he met an old street acquaintance, — Jim Nolan.

"How are you, Sam?" said Jim.

"Tip-top!" answered Sam.

"Where do you keep yourself? Are you blackin' boots, now?"

"No," answered Sam, with rather an important air. "I'm in an office."

"How much do you get?"

"Four dollars a week."

"That's good. How'd you get it?"

"Oh, the doctor took a fancy to me, and asked me to come."

"You're in luck. So you're with a doctor?"

"Yes, — Dr. Graham. He's a corn-doctor."

"Where does he hang out?"

"No. —, Broadway."

"Do you have much to do?"

"Not very much."

"How do you come down here, then?"

"I'm takin' a letter to Brooklyn for the doctor."

"Are you?"

"Yes," said Sam; adding unluckily, "There s money in it."

"Is there?" said Jim, pricking up his ears. "How do you know? Let's see the letter."

Sam took the letter from his inside coat-pocket, and passed it to Jim.

The latter held it up to the light, and tried to look inside. Fortune favored his efforts. The envelope was imperfectly fastened, and came open.

"There, Jim," said Sam, "now see what you've done."

"Let's look inside, and see how much money there is," suggested Jim.

Sam hesitated.

"It won't do any harm to look at it," said the tempter.

"That's so," said Sam.

He accordingly drew out the enclosure, and disclosed two ten-dollar bills.

Jim's eyes sparkled with greed.

"Twenty dollars!" he exclaimed. "What a lot of good that would do us!"

Sam's principles were not firm, but he had a good place, and the temptation was not as strong as in Jim's case; so he answered, "Maybe it would, but it aint ours."

Jim fastened his little black eyes on Sam cunningly.

"It might be," he answered.

"How could it be?"

"You could keep it."

"The doctor'd find it out."

"Tell him somebody hooked it out of your pocket. He wouldn't know."

Sam shook his head.

"I aint goin' to lose a good place just for that," he said.

"Think what a lot of things you could do for ten dollars," urged Jim.

"Twenty, you mean."

"That's ten apiece, isn't it?"

"Oh, you want some, do you?" inquired Sam.

"Yes; I'll take it from you, and then give you back half. So, it'll be me that stole it. They can't do nothin' to you. Come, I'll go over to Brooklyn with you, and then you can make up your mind."

On board the boat Jim renewed his persuasions, and finally Sam yielded.

"I'm afraid the doctor'll think I took it," he said.

"No matter! He can't prove nothin'."

"We'll find it hard to change the bills."

"No we won't. I'll tell you where to go. Can you play billiards?"

"No; but I'd like to learn."

"I know, and I'll learn you. There's a saloon over in Brooklyn where we can go and have a game. We'll pay out of one of the bills."

Now Sam had long wanted to learn the game of billiards, and this seemed a good opportunity. Perhaps this consideration as much as any determined him to close with his friend's proposal. When, therefore, they had reached the Brooklyn side, instead of taking the horse-cars to Dr. Graham's house, Sam followed his companion to a low billiard saloon not far away.

There were four tables, one of which only was occupied, for it was too early. On one side of the room was a bar, behind which stood a man in his shirt-sleeves.

"Well, boys, what do you want?" he asked.

"We want a table," said Jim. "We're goin' to play a game."

The man in the shirt-sleeves produced, from underneath the counter, a green pasteboard box containing four ivory billiard balls.

"What table will you have?" he asked.

"This one here," said Jim, leading the way to one farthest from the door.

"Now take a cue, Sam," he said. "We'll have a jolly game."

"You must tell me how to play."

"Oh, I'll learn you."

Jim was not a very skilful player, but he knew something about the game, and under his instruction Sam made some progress, being able to make a shot now and then. He was very much pleased with the game, and determined to devote his spare earnings to this form of recreation hereafter. When the game was ended, a full hour had passed.

"I didn't think it was so late," said Sam, starting. "I shall have to go."

"Go and pay for the game first."

"You ought to pay half."

"No; I beat. The one that loses the game has to pay."

"Of course you beat. It was my first game."

"Never mind. You'll soon play as well as I, and then I shall have to pay half the time."

"Do you think I'll improve?"

"Of course you will. We'll play again to-night."

"Here?"

"No, in New York. I'll show you a good saloon in Chatham street."

Sam stepped up to the counter.

"How much do you want?" he asked.

"Sixty cents."

"It's only twenty-five cents a game," said Jim Nolan.

"Your game was longer than two ordinary ones. I'll call it fifty cents."

Sam produced the ten-dollar bill, and received in return nine dollars and a half. The clerk was rather surprised at a boy presenting so large a bill. He suspected that it was not come by honestly; but, as he argued, that was none of his business. What he cared for most was to get paid for the billiards. So Sam, who had felt a little uneasy about offering the money, was more at his ease.

"We had a good game, didn't we?" said Jim.

"Yes," said Sam.

"And you did bully for the first time. I couldn't play so well my first game."

Sam felt flattered by this compliment from his companion.

"Now I must go back," he said.

"I'll go along back with you. But we'll take a drink first. I want to change my bill too."

"Why didn't you do it in the billiard-saloon? They had a bar there."

"They might suspect something if both of us offered tens. Here's a place close by. Come in here."

Jim led the way into a drinking-saloon, and Sam followed.

"It's my treat," said Jim. "What'll you have?"

"What are you goin' to take?"

"A whiskey-punch."

"I'll take one too."

"Two whiskey-punches, and mind you make 'em stiff," said Jim.

He tossed down his glass, but Sam drank more slowly.

Jim paid for the drinks, and they went out into the street.

CHAPTER XXIV.

SAM'S EXCUSES.

SAM was not used to liquor, and was more easily affected than most. When he got out into the street his head spun round, and he staggered. His companion observed it.

"Why, you don't mean ter say yer tight, Sam?" he said, pausing and looking at him.

"I don't know what it is," said Sam, "but I feel queer."

"Kinder light in the head, and shaky in the legs?"

"Yes, that's the way I feel."

"Then you're drunk."

"Drunk!" ejaculated Sam, rather frightened, for he was still unsophisticated compared with his companion.

"Just so. I say, you must be a chicken to get

tight on one whiskey-punch," added Jim, rather contemptuously.

"It was strong," said Sam, by way of apology, leaning against a lamp-post for support.

"It was stiffish," said Jim. "I always take 'em so."

"And don't you feel it at all?" queried Sam.

"Not a bit," said Jim, decidedly. "I aint a baby."

"Nor I either," said Sam, with a spark of his accustomed spirit. "Only I aint used to it."

"Why, I could take three glasses, one after the other, without gettin' tight," said Jim, proudly. "I tell you, I've got a strong stomach."

"I wish I hadn't taken the drink," said Sam. "When will I feel better?"

"In an hour or two."

"I can't go back to the doctor this way. He'll know I've been drinkin'. I wish I could lie down somewhere."

"I'll tell you what. Come round to the ferry-room. You can sit down there till you feel better."

"Give me your arm, Jim. I'm light-headed."

With Jim's assistance Sam made his way to Fulton Ferry, but instead of going over in the next boat he leaned back in his seat in the waiting-room, and rested. Jim walked about on the pier, his hands in his pocket, with an independent air. He felt happy and prosperous. Never before in his life, probably, had he had so much money in his possession. Some men with a hundred thousand dollars would have felt poorer than Jim with nine dollars and a half.

By and by Sam felt enough better to start on his homeward journey. Jim agreed to accompany him as far as the New York side.

"I don't know what the doctor will say when he finds out the money is gone," said Sam, soberly.

"You just tell him it was stolen from you by a pickpocket."

"Suppose he don't believe it?"

"He can't prove nothin'."

"He might search me."

"So he might," said Jim. "I'll tell you what you'd better do."

"What?"

"Just give me the money to keep for you. Then if he searches you, he won't find it."

If Jim expected this suggestion to be adopted, he undervalued Sam's shrewdness. That young man had not knocked about the streets eight months for nothing.

"I guess not," said Sam, significantly. "Maybe I wouldn't find it any easier if you took it."

"You don't call me a thief, do you?" demanded Jim, offended.

"It looks as if we was both thieves," said Sam, candidly.

"You needn't talk so loud," said Jim, hurriedly. "There's no use in tellin' everybody that I see. I don't want the money, only, if the old man finds it, don't blame me."

"You needn't be mad, Jim," said Sam. "I'll need the money myself. I guess I'll have to hide it."

"Do you wear stockin's?" asked Jim.

"Yes; don't you?"

"Not in warm weather. They aint no good. They only get dirty. But if you wear 'em, that's the place to hide the money."

"I guess you're right," said Sam. "I wouldn't have thought of it. Where can I do it?"

"Wait till we're on the New York side. You can sit down on one of the piers and do it. Nobody'll see you."

Sam thought this good advice, and decided to follow it.

"There is some use in stockin's," said Jim, reflectively. "If I was in your place, I wouldn't know where to stow away the money. Where are you goin' now?"

"I'll have to go back," said Sam. "I've been a long time already."

"I'm goin' to get some dinner," said Jim.

"I haven't got time," said Sam. "Besides, I don't feel so hungry as usual. I guess it's the drink I took."

"It don't take away my appetite," said his companion, with an air of superiority.

Sam took the cars home. Knowing what he did, it was with an uncomfortable feeling that he ascended the stairs and entered the presence of Dr. Graham.

The doctor looked angry.

"What made you so long?" he demanded abruptly. "Did you find the house?"

"No," answered Sam, wishing that his embarrassing explanations were fully over. "No, I didn't."

"You didn't find the house!" exclaimed the doctor, in angry surprise. "Why didn't you?"

"I thought it wasn't any use," stammered Sam.

"Wasn't any use!" repeated the chiropodist. "Explain yourself, sir, at once."

"As long as I hadn't got the letter," proceeded Sam

Now the secret was out.

"What did you do with the letter?" demanded Dr. Graham, suspiciously.

"I lost it."

"Lost it! How could you lose it? Did you know there was money in it?" said his employer, looking angry and disturbed.

"Yes, sir; you said so."

"Then why were you not careful of it, you young rascal?"

"I was, sir; that is, I tried to be. But it was stolen."

"Who would steal the letter unless he knew that it contained money?"

"That's it, sir. I ought not to have told anybody."

"Sit down, and tell me all about it, or it will be the worse for you," said the doctor.

"Now for it!" thought Sam.

"You see, sir," he commenced, "I was in the horse-cars in Brooklyn, when I saw a boy I knew. We got to talking, and, before I knew it, I told him that I was carryin' a letter with money in it. I took it out of my coat-pocket, and showed it to him."

"You had no business to do it," said Dr. Graham. "No one but a fool would show a money-letter. So the boy stole it, did he?"

"Oh, no," said Sam, hastily. "It wasn't he."

"Who was it, then? Don't be all day telling your story," said the doctor, irritably.

"There was a young man sitting on the other side of me," said Sam. "He was well-dressed, and I didn't think he'd do such a thing; but he must have stole the letter."

"What makes you think so?"

"He got out only two or three minutes afterwards, and it wasn't long after that that I missed the letter."

"What did you do?"

"I stopped the car, and went back. Jim went back along with me. We looked all round, tryin' to find the man, but we couldn't."

"Of course you couldn't," growled the doctor. "Did you think he would stay till you came up?"

"No, sir. That is, I didn't know what to think. I felt so bad about losing the money," said Sam, artfully.

Now this story was on the whole very well got up. It did not do credit to Sam's principles, but it did do credit to his powers of invention. It might be true. There are such men as pickpockets to be found riding in our city horse-cars, as possibly some of my readers may have occasion to know. As yet Dr. Graham did not doubt the story of his young assistant. Sam came very near getting off scot-free.

"But for your carelessness this money would not have been lost," said his employer. "You ought to make up the loss to me."

"I haven't got any money," said Sam.

A sudden thought came to Dr. Graham. "Empty your pockets," he said.

"How lucky I put the bills in my stocking!" thought Sam.

He turned out his pockets, disclosing fifty cents. It was Friday, and to-morrow his weekly wages would come due.

"That's all I've got," he said.

"Twenty dollars is five weeks' salary," said Dr. Graham. "You ought to work for me five weeks without pay."

"I'd starve to death," said Sam, in alarm. "I wouldn't be able to buy anything to eat."

"I can keep back part of your salary, then," said his employer. "It is only proper that you should suffer for your negligence."

At this moment a friend of the doctor's entered the office.

"What is the matter?" he asked.

Dr. Graham explained briefly.

"Perhaps," said the visitor, "I can throw some light upon your loss."

"You! How?"

"I happened to be coming over from Brooklyn an hour since on the same boat with that young man there," he said, quietly.

Sam turned pale. There was something in the speaker's tone that frightened him.

CHAPTER XXV.

BROUGHT TO JUSTICE.

Sam would have been glad to leave the office, but he knew that to ask would be to subject him to increased suspicion. Besides, the stranger might not be intending to accuse him.

Dr. Graham's attention was excited, and he asked, "Do you know anything of this matter, Mr. Clement?"

"Yes, doctor. As I said, I was on board the Brooklyn ferry with this young man and a friend of his, whom I believe he addressed as Jim. I heard them talk, being in the next seat, about money, and something was said about concealment. My curiosity was aroused, and I made up my mind to follow them after they left the boat."

"He knows all about it," thought Sam. "I wish I hadn't come back."

"Go on," said Dr. Graham, eying Sam sternly as he spoke. "You followed the boys?"

"Yes. They made their way to the end of a pier, where this young man of yours slipped off his stockings, and, as well as I could tell, for I was watching at a distance, concealed some bills in them, and afterwards drew them on again. It struck me at once that if the money had been honestly come by, they wouldn't have been so anxious to secrete it."

"Sam," said the doctor, sternly, "what have you to say to this charge?"

"It was my money," stammered Sam.

"What did you put it in your stockings for?"

"Jim told me how dangerous it was to carry it round in my pocket loose. So, as I hadn't any pocket-book, I put it in my stockings."

"Very probable, indeed. Suppose you take off your stockings."

Sam had decided objections to this; but he saw that it would be of no use to urge them, and slowly and reluctantly complied.

"Now put in your hand, and take out the money."

Sam did so.

The doctor counted the bills.

"Here are only nine dollars," he said. "Take out the rest."

"There isn't any more," said Sam.

"Don't attempt to deceive me," said his employer, sternly. "It will be the worse for you if you do."

"There isn't any more," persisted Sam, earnestly. "If you don't believe it, you may look yourself."

Dr. Graham did so, and found the statement correct.

"There were twenty dollars in the letter," he said, sternly. "What has become of the other eleven?"

There was no use in persisting in denial further, and Sam made a virtue of necessity.

"Jim got half the money," he confessed.

"Who's Jim?"

"Jim Nolan."

"How came he to get half the money? Did you owe it to him?"

For the first time it struck Sam that he had been a fool to give away ten dollars without adequate return. All that Jim had given him was bad advice, which is never worth taking.

"I don't know how I came to give it to him," said Sam. "It was he who wanted me to take the money. I wouldn't have done it but for Jim."

"It strikes me," said Mr. Clement, "that Jim is not a very desirable companion. So you gave him ten dollars?"

"Yes, sir."

"Did you spend any of the money?" asked Dr. Graham.

"Yes, sir."

"In what way?"

"I went in with Jim, and played a game of billiards."

"Paying for the game with my money?"

"Yes, sir."

"What else?"

"Jim took me into a drinking-place, and treated me to a whiskey-punch."

"Also with my money, I suppose."

"Yes, sir; he wanted to get the ten-dollar bill changed."

"Was this in Brooklyn or New York?"

"In Brooklyn."

"Upon my word, very well planned. So you expected me to believe your story about having your pocket picked. Did you?"

"Yes, sir."

"A pretty story, Mr. Clement," said the doctor, turning to his friend. "What would you advise me to do, — arrest the boy?"

"Oh, don't," implored Sam, turning pale; "I'll never do it again."

"You won't have the chance," said the doctor, drily.

"If you ask my advice," said Mr. Clement, "I will give it. I suspect this Jim is the worse boy of the two. Now he's got ten dollars of your money."

"Yes, sir."

"Do you mean to let him keep it?"

"He's spent part of it by this time."

"You can get the rest back."

"How? I don't know the boy."

"You know his name. The Superintendent of the

Newsboys' Lodging House could probably put you on his track. Besides, your boy here can help you."

"I don't know but you are right."

"Sam," said Mr. Clement, "are you willing to help Dr. Graham get back his money?"

"I don't like to get Jim into a scrape," said Sam.

"It seems he's got you into a scrape. It is your only chance of escaping being sent to Blackwell's Island."

"Will Jim be sent there?"

"That depends on the doctor. If this Jim will give back what he has of the money you gave him, and agree to give back the rest as soon as he earns it, I think the doctor will let him off."

"Then I'll do what I can," said Sam.

"As for you," said the doctor, "I shall retain these nine dollars; also the four I was to have paid you to-morrow. If I get back the full amount from your confederate, I will pay you the difference. Now how can you get at this Jim?"

"He'll be somewhere around City Hall Park," said Sam.

"You may go in search of him. Tell him to come

to this office with you. If he don't come he will be arrested, and I will have no mercy upon him. If you undertake to play me false, the same fate awaits you."

"Don't be afraid," said Sam. "I'll come back, honor bright!"

"Do you think he will?" asked Dr. Graham, turning to Mr. Clement.

"Yes, for he knows it wouldn't be safe for him to stay away."

"Go away, then, and come back as soon as possible."

Sam made all haste to the City Hall Park, where he expected to find Jim. He was not disappointed. Jim was sitting on one of the steps of the City Hall smoking a cigar. He had the air of a gentleman of leisure and independent income, with no cares to disturb or harass him.

He did not see Sam till the latter called him by name.

"Where'd you come from, Sam?" he asked, placidly.

"From the office."

"Did the boss make a row about the money?"

"You bet he did!"

"He didn't find out, did he?"

"Yes, he did."

Jim looked up now.

"He don't know anything about me does he?" he inquired.

"I had to tell him."

"That's mean!" exclaimed Jim. "You'd ought to be ashamed to tell on a friend."

"I had to. There was a chap — a friend of the doctor's — that was on the boat, and heard us talkin' about the money. He followed us, and saw me stuff the money in my stockin'."

Jim indulged in a profane ejaculation.

"What's he goin' to do about it?" he asked.

"He's made me give up the money, and he's sent me for you."

"I won't go," said Jim, hastily.

"You'd better. If you don't, you'll be took up."

"What am I to go to the office for?" asked Jim, rather startled.

"To give up the money."

"I've spent two dollars."

"If you give up what's left, and agree to pay the rest, he'll let you off."

"Did he say so?"

"Yes, he told me so."

If there had been any hope of escaping with the money, Jim would have declined calling on Dr. Graham; but of that he knew there was little chance. Indeed, he was not altogether unknown to the police, having, on two or three previous occasions, come under their notice. So, considerably less cheerful than before, he accompanied Sam to the office.

"Is this the boy?" asked the doctor, surveying Sam's companion attentively.

"Yes, sir."

"I am glad to see you, young man," said the doctor, drily. "Suppose we settle money matters first of all. How much have you left?"

Jim drew out eight dollars in bills.

"So far, so good. You owe me two dollars."

"Yes, sir."

"I won't ask for your note of hand. I'm afraid I couldn't negotiate it; but I expect you to pay me back the balance by instalments. If not, I shall know where to lay hold of you."

Jim had nothing to say.

"Now you can go. Sam, you can stay."

"I suppose he's goin' to send me off," thought Sam.

"You may stay till to-morrow night, Sam," said the doctor, "and I will pay you what balance I owe you. After that, I think we had better part company. You are a little too enterprising for me."

Sam made no objection. In fact, he had got tired of the confinement, and thought it would be an agreeable variety to return to his old life again. The next evening, therefore, he retired from professional life, and, with a balance of fifty cents in his possession, set up once more as a street vagabond. When Jim Nolan paid up his indebtedness, he would be entitled to two dollars more. Until then he was held for the debt of his confederate.

CHAPTER XXVI.

PIPKIN'S DINING-ROOMS.

SUNDAY is a dull day with the street-boys, whatever their business may be. The boot-blacks lose least, but if the day be unpropitious their earnings are small. On such a day the Newsboys' Lodge is a great resource. It supplies all that a boy actually needs — lodging and two meals — for the small sum of eighteen cents, and in cases of need will trust boys to that amount.

Sam naturally had recourse to this hold on finding himself out of a situation. He had enough to pay his expenses, and did not feel compelled to go to work till Monday. Monday morning, however, the reduced state of his finances compelled him to look for employment. If he had had a little capital he might have set up as a newsboy or boot-black, but five cents can hardly be considered sufficient capital for either of these lines of business. Credit is the next best thing to capital, but Sam had no credit. He found that out, after an ineffectual attempt to borrow money of a boot-black, who, having ten dollars in a savings-bank, was regarded in his own class with high respect as a wealthy capitalist. The name of this exceptional young man was William Clark, better known among the boys as Ready Money Bill.

When twelve o'clock came, and Sam had earned nothing, he bethought himself of Bill, the capitalist.

"Bill," he said, "I want to borrer a dollar."

"You do!" said Bill, sharply. "What for?"

"To set me up in business."

"What business?"

"Evenin' papers."

"Haven't you got no stamps?"

"No."

"What have you been doin'?"

"I've been in an office."

"Why didn't you stay?"

"The boss thought he wouldn't need me no longer."

"I see," said Bill, nodding. "You got sacked."

"Not exactly."

"Same thing."

"Will you lend me the money?"

"I'd never get it back ag'in."

"Yes, you would."

"I dunno about that. Where'd you get money to pay me back?"

"The boss owes me two dollars."

"Why don't he pay you?"

"One of my friends cheated him out of it, and he won't pay me till it's paid back."

"Maybe he won't pay it back."

"Yes, he will. Will you lend me the money?"

"No, I won't. You'd ought to have saved money like I have."

"I'd have had two dollars, if Jim hadn't stolen money."

"That aint my fault. I aint goin' to lose my money for you. You can save like I do."

Bill was right, no doubt. He was a bee, and Sam was a drone, and the drones are always ready to avail themselves of the accumulations of their more industrious brothers.

Sam began to feel hungry. However irregular he might be in other ways, his appetite was surprisingly regular. He paused in front of a restaurant, and looked wistfully in at the windows.

"I wish I was a waiter," he thought. "They have all they want to eat every day."

It will be seen that Sam's ambition was not a lofty one. But then he was practical enough to see that three square meals a day are more to be desired than empty fame.

As he was standing at the window a man from within came to the door. Being without a hat, Sam supposed him to be connected with the restaurant, as, indeed, he was. Sam drew back, supposing that he was to be sent off. But here he was mistaken.

"Come here, Johnny," said the proprietor, for it was the owner of the restaurant who addressed our hero.

Sam approached wondering.

"Have you had dinner?"

"No," said Sam, promptly.

"Would you like some?"

Sam's answer, in the affirmative, was equally prompt.

"But you haven't any money, eh?"

"That's so," said Sam. "Wonder how he found out?" he thought.

"We don't give away dinners, but you can earn one," said Mr. Pipkin, for it was Pipkin's restaurant.

"Do you want me for a waiter?" asked Sam, hopefully.

"No; you wouldn't do. You haven't had experience. I want a boy to distribute handbills in front of the saloon. Can you do that?"

"Yes, I can," said Sam, eagerly. "I've done that before."

"All right. Come in."

Sam entered. He hoped that a preliminary dinner would be offered him, but Mr. Pipkin was not in the habit of paying in advance, and, perhaps, he was right. He brought forward a pile of circulars about the same size as Dr. Graham's, and handed them to Sam.

"I've just opened a new saloon," he said, "and I

want to invite the patronage of the public. Stand here, and distribute these to the passers-by."

"All right," said Sam. "When will you give me some dinner?"

"In about an hour. This is the time when people generally dine, and I want to catch as many as I can."

Sam read one of the circulars rapidly.

This is the way it read: —

"PIPKIN'S DINING-ROOMS.

Unsurpassed for the excellence of cookery, and the cheapness of prices.

Call once,

And you will be sure to come again."

"I'm goin' to come once, and I'll call again if they'll let me," said Sam to himself.

In about an hour he was called in. The customers had thinned out, but there were a few at the tables. Sam was directed to sit down at a table in the back part of the room.

"Now, then," said the waiter, "hurry up, young 'un, and tell us what you want."

"Roast turkey and cranberry sauce," ordered Sam.

"All out. Try again," was the laconic reply.

"Roast chicken."

"That's all out too."

Sam looked disappointed.

"Oyster stew."

"All out."

"Is everything out?"

"No; there's some roast veal, unless you prefer hash."

"I don't like hash," said Sam, decidedly. "Bring on your veal, and don't forget the potatoes, and some bread and butter."

"You've got a healthy appetite," said the waiter.

"You bet I have, and I've a right to it. I've earned my dinner, and I want it."

The articles he had ordered were brought, and he attacked them with vigor. Then he called for a second course.

"A piece of mince-pie."

"All out," said the waiter.

"Apple-pie."

"That's out."

"I guess your customers all had healthy appetites to-day," said Sam. "Bring on something or other, and mind you bring enough of it."

A plate of rice-pudding was set before him, and speedily appropriated. He tried to get a second plate, but his application was unsuccessful. He was given to understand that he was entitled to only one plate, and was forced to rise from the table not wholly satisfied.

CHAPTER XXVII.

CONCLUSION.

SAM did not retain his new position long. A week later he was dismissed. Though no reason was assigned, the proprietor probably thought it better to engage a boy with a smaller appetite. But Sam was by no means discouraged. He was more self-reliant than when nearly a year before he entered the city, and more confident of rubbing along somehow. If he could not sell papers, he could black boots. If wholly without capital, he could haunt the neighborhood of the piers, and seek employment as a baggage-smasher.

For the next two years it will be unnecessary to detail Sam's experiences. They did not differ materially from those of other street-boys, — now a day of plenty, now of want, now a stroke of luck, which made him feel rich as a millionnaire, now a season of bad fortune. Day by day, and week by week, his recollections of his country home became more vague, and he could hardly realize that he had ever lived anywhere else than in the streets of New York. It was at this time that the unexpected encounter with Deacon Hopkins brought back the memories of his early life, and led him to contrast them curiously with his present experiences. There did not seem much for Sam to be proud of, ragged vagabond as he was; but for all that he looked down upon his former self with ineffable contempt.

"What a greenhorn I was when I first came to the city!" he reflected. "How easy I was took in! I didn't know nothin' about life then. How sick I was when I smoked my first cigar! Now, I can smoke half a dozen, one after the other, only I can't raise the stamps to buy 'em. How I fooled the deacon, though!" and Sam laughed in hearty enjoyment of the joke. "I wonder what'll he say of me when he gets back."

Sam plunged his hands deep down into his pockets. There was nothing to hinder, for, as usual, they were empty. He had spent the small amount obtained from the deacon, and he was just even with the world. He had neither debts nor assets. He had only daily recurring wants, and these he was not always able to supply.

It was in the afternoon of the day made memorable by his interview with the deacon that another adventure befell Sam. As it exhibits him in a more favorable light than usual, I am glad to chronicle it.

He was lounging about, waiting for something to turn up, when he felt a little hand slipped into his, and heard a small voice pleading, "Take me home. I'm lost."

Sam looked down in surprise to find his hand clasped by a little boy, apparently about four years of age. What attracted him to Sam is uncertain. Possibly his face seemed familiar to the little boy.

"What's your name, Johnny?" asked Sam, gently.

"My name aint Johnny; it's Bertie," said the little boy.

"What's your other name?"

"Dalton."

"Bertie Dalton?"

"Yes. I want to go home."

"So you shall," said Sam, good-naturedly, "if you'll tell me where you live."

"Don't you know?" asked Bertie.

"No."

"I thought you did," said Bertie, disappointed. "I want to go home to mamma."

Sam was puzzled.

"How did you come to be lost?" he asked.

"I went out with Marie—that's the nurse—and when she was talking with another nurse I went to play. Then I couldn't find her, and I'm so frightened."

"Don't be frightened, Bertie," said Sam, gently; for his heart was drawn to the little fellow. "I guess I'll find your home. Let me guess. Do you live in Twentieth street?"

Bertie shook his head.

"Where were you playing?"

"In the Park."

"It must be Union Park," thought Sam.

An idea struck him. He went into a neighboring druggist's, and, asking for a directory, turned to the list of Daltons. There was only one living near

Union Park; this one lived on Fourteenth street, between Sixth and Seventh avenues. Sam decided to take the child into this street, and see if he recognized it. The experiment proved successful. Arrived in the street the child cried joyfully: —

"This is where I live."

"Can you find the house?"

"Yes; it's right on," said Bertie.

In brief, Sam took Bertie home. He found the family in great distress. The nurse had returned, and declared incoherently that Master Bertie had been carried off, and she couldn't find him anywhere. A message was about to be sent to the police when the young truant was brought home. The mother clasped him fondly in her arms, and kissed him many times. Then she bethought herself of Sam.

"How can I thank you," she said gratefully, "for bringing my darling home?"

"Oh, it's nothing," said Sam. "I was afraid at first I couldn't find where he lived; but he told me his name, and I looked in the directory."

Mrs. Dalton saw that Sam was ragged, and her grateful heart prompted her to do something for him.

"Have you any place?" she asked.

"No," said Sam.

"Wouldn't you like one?"

"Yes, I should," said Sam, promptly. "It's hard work getting a living about the streets."

"It must be," said the lady, with sympathy. "Have you no friends?"

"None, except poor boys like I am."

"You have been kind to my dear Bertie, and I want to do something to show my gratitude. Without you I shudder to think what might have become of him."

"Nobody'd hurt a little chap like him," said Sam.

"They might steal him," said Mrs. Dalton. "Have you had any dinner?"

"No, ma'am."

"Come into the house. Maggie, see that this boy has a good meal. Take care of him till Mr. Dalton comes home. Then I will see what can be done for him."

"All right, mum."

Sam had no objections to this arrangement. He

was never at a loss for an appetite, and the prospect was an attractive one. He made himself at home in the kitchen, where his rescue of little Bertie and the evident favor of Mrs. Dalton made him the recipient of much attention. He felt that he was in luck for once in his life, and was convinced of it when, on the arrival of Mr. Dalton, he was offered the post of errand-boy at five dollars a week, with a present of five dollars in advance. He asked no time for consideration, but accepted at once.

"You may report for service to-morrow morning," said Mr. Dalton. "There is my business-card. Can you find it?"

"I know where it is," said Sam. "I'll be there."

Sam's chance had come. He was invited to fill an humble but respectable position. Would he give satisfaction, or drift back after a while to his vagabond habits? Young outlaw as he had been, was he likely to grow into an orderly member of society? If any of my readers are curious on this subject, they are referred to the next volume of this series, entitled

SAM'S CHANCE;

AND HOW HE IMPROVED IT.

Milton Keynes UK
Ingram Content Group UK Ltd.
UKHW042309160224
437951UK00004B/342

9 783382 832728